HOT BULLETS FOR LOVE

By
GENTRY NYLAND

Chapter One

T
HE BAROMETER DROPPED. For the first time in years the hurricane warning was to be seen atop the Whitehall Building. A fifty-mile gale, blown in from the Southeast, swept the chilling rain across Manhattan.

Joe South, seated by the window, stared at the opposite office building as the howling wind threatened to crash the rattling casement and shatter the quiet interior of the too-dignified office. He scowled and decided that all lawyers were either crooks or fools, and he knew from past experience that the man across the desk from him was not a fool.

Joe had been feeling good when he arrived at the lawyer's office an hour ago. He was wearing his dark blue suit with a white shirt and black tie. He thought he looked neat and respectable and had expected to merit some recognition of this virtuous conduct from Van Pelt. But no. He had had to kick his heels in the reception room twenty minutes while some female client poured her troubles into the lawyer's too-willing ear.

From the musical overtones of the finishing-school voice Joe didn't blame the lawyer, but the enforced wait hadn't improved his own temper. She must be one of Van Pelt's "specials" to rate the private entrance.

He scowled at the water slapping against the window panes. Even now, after forty minutes closeted with one of the largest corporation lawyers in Manhattan, he knew very little more about the job he had been hired for than when he came in. Apparently all it amounted to was to bodyguard some rich brat to the tune of three hundred and fifty dollars a month. He, Joe Smith, the best private detective in New York, had come to this. Oh, well, he had to eat, and since his license had been suspended as a result of his activities in the Martin kidnaping case he couldn't be choosy.

Van Pelt's voice broke into his brooding.

"And remember this, Joe," the crisp words were impatient. "This is a respectable firm and I hope you will try to conduct yourself accordingly."

Stuyvesant Van Pelt's person was like his name. He was a tall, thin, ascetic man in his early fifties. His cold blue eyes were remote and steely, and he wore a small, waxed military mustache over slightly full lips which might have suggested a weakness for the fleshpots.

Seated now behind a massive desk, he looked and acted like the headmaster of an exclusive boys' school. The wide expanse of polished glass in front of him was free of all standard office equipment

3

Instead there was a fifth bottle of Scotch, a syphon of seltzer and two glasses arranged neatly on a silver tray.

Joe frowned and removed his chubby leg from the arm of the chair. He reached for the bottle, and ignoring the seltzer, poured three ounces of Scotch and swallowed it neat. He lit a cigarette and blew smoke ceilingward as he relaxed in his former position.

The lawyer shifted his position and coughed.

"I must remind you also, Joe, that this job, if you take it, will not call for your usual amount of drinking."

Joe's expression of bored indifference didn't change.

"It's the rain," he mourned. "I'm just like a woman. Every time I hear water running I hafta drink." He looked at the lawyer through sleepy lids and added softly, "How much?"

"My client," Van Pelt told him, "has provided a substantial retainer. I might add, unusually substantial, considering the nature of the case. The sum mentioned in the letter I sent you was seven hundred dollars, and the job should be satisfactorily completed within two months. I think that is unusually substantial, and, of course, if Mr. Raleigh should want you for longer you will be proportionately imbursed."

Joe said, "It's substantial," and extended a chubby hand. The lawyer started to take it, then realizing the absurdity of the gesture his hand went to his pocket instead. From there he took a manila envelope and placed it in Joe's outstretched palm. The detective slit it quickly and took out seven hundred-dollar bills. He counted them carefully and slipped them into his own pocket.

"I assume then," Van Pelt said, "that you will begin work tonight. I have told Mr. Raleigh you would see him at three-thirty this afternoon at Hillman Hospital."

Joe said, "Yeah," and heaved himself to his feet. He threw his raincoat over his arm and started for the door. Halfway there Van Pelt's voice stopped him.

"Just one thing more," he was saying, "it's my opinion that this assignment could be better handled without the assistance of . . . er . . . ah . . . shall I say, your confederates?"

"Okay," Joe said over his shoulder. "It don't look like I'll need 'em anyway. S'long."

In the outer office he stopped before the girl at the typewriter. The name plate on her desk said she was Miss Lane.

"Hello, Beacon Hill," Joe greeted her and stopped beside the desk.

"Oh, hello, Joe. Gosh, you scared me." She took off her glasses and looked him up and down. "Do you know, Joey, you're getting to be more like Jack Oakie every time I see you?"

"That's not original, baby, and don't think you're flattering me. How's tricks with Van Pelt?"

The elevator opened directly into the reception room and he pressed the down button. The girl at the desk looked at him suspiciously.

"You've just been in there. You should know."

Joe leered. "I don't but I can guess."

The red line of her lips parted to reveal small, even teeth. "That alleged mind of yours needs a trip to the laundry, Joe South," she hissed.

"Now, now, shug, you walked smack into that one," Joe countered as the elevator door opened. "Remember? Suspicion is my business." The pen she had picked up cracked against the outside of the cage. Some of the ink splashed the detective's shirt. It was red. He was chuckling as the elevator door closed behind him.

As he swung through the door into the street a blast of wind swept off his hat and kicked it several blocks down Broadway. He didn't bother to chase it. Rain drenched him as he ran for the only cab parked on the street. Joe climbed in.

"Take me to the hotel," he ordered.

Traffic up Broadway was almost at a standstill. Progress was a fitful series of gears grinding and brakes screeching. The cab swung left at Times Square and stopped in front of the Brant Hotel. Joe slammed the door and started across the street. The driver honked his horn and yelled.

"Hey, Joey. Not so fast. You owe me fifteen dollars and eighty cents."

Joe came back. Without a word he took out the envelope Van Pelt had given him and solemnly handed one of the hundred-dollar bills to the driver. The boy blinked and swore.

"Holy cats, Joey! Who d'ya think I'm drivin' for? Brink's Express!"

"All right now, dope," Joe grinned. "Keep your shirt on. I'll have your change later."

He replaced the envelope and hurried into the lobby. The clerk at the desk handed him three bills and a telephone message. The message was from May. Joe hummed to himself as he read it in the elevator. It said:

> *Goggles happier and fatter and much better company. We both hope you keep away for a while.*

He scowled and stuffed the note in his pocket. Goggles. That smut-smeared Siamese.

As he opened the door to his room, one of the two men who

had been lounging on the bed got up. He was a good-looking red-headed boy except for a nose that looked like something the Germans did to Poland. Contact with leather had also failed to improve his left ear. He had freckled, healthy skin and his blue eyes were clear and guileless. The grin he gave Joe as he entered revealed large glistening teeth. He was naked except for a pair of athletic trunks. His name was James Michael Kierney. Joe liked him.

The other man was different. He didn't rise, but one side of his mouth lifted in a brief grin as he said, "Cheer-o." If James Michael Kierney looked like a well-thumped punching bag David Kitchener Carton was the life-size dream picture of every blonde, brunette and red-head from Passamaquoddy to San Francisco Bay. Six feet two, with dark hair graying at the temples, "Kitch" Carton was the composite of Anthony Eden and Ronald Colman in a rôle designed for Lawrence of Arabia. His accent was clipped close to ground that had never seen Harvard Yard. His age might have been anything from thirty-five to forty-five.

Kierney spied the red spots on Joe's shirt.

"So you been catchin' 'em on the old shnozola, huh? Who hung that one on you, Joey? Did that high-class mouthpiece get tough?"

Joe looked patronizing.

"My boy, you've left so many of your fine, virile corpuscles in the rings of second-rate prelims you haven't enough blood left to recognize it when you see it. This isn't blood, slap-happy. This is ink. Red ink. Van Pelt only makes passes at people with skirts on."

Carton grinned.

"So we're still in the red? Inconsiderate of you to go about displaying our financial status on your shirt front."

Joe shrugged and sat on the edge of the bed.

"Listen, boys," he pleaded. "How many times do I have to tell you there's a swell strike over in Jersey praying for guys like you. Eight bucks a day for walking scabs through picket lines. The only place those dumb strikers ever think of heaving a brick is at your heads. It'll be a push-over for you."

Kierney removed the cap from the rye and held it under the detective's nose. "See this, Joey? When you're ready to talk you get a swig of it. How's about it?"

Joe said, "All right. Gimme it." He took a long drink, winced and leaned back against the foot of the bed. He hesitated, scowled at each of them and began, "It's like this . . ."

"It is like hell," Kierney snapped. "We want the straight dope, Joey."

"I'm giving it to you, but for cripe's sake stop calling me Joey.

It's just a simple job of playing bodyguard to a Little Lord Fauntleroy who's been matching pennies with the gang from the wrong side of the tracks."

Carton said, "Guarding him from what?"

"Everything and anything. The kid's a fugitive from the Blue Book and the family's trying to hook him back on the leash. You can't blame the kid for that, but he's doing it the wrong way. This guy apparently sets up all the pins in the Social Register, then steps back and bowls them over. According to Van Pelt he's been seen around in the hot spots with a couple of hoods for the past year. That's a part of my job. To keep him away from them—or see that he keeps ticking while he's with them."

"And the other part?"

"What do you think? A dame, of course. There aren't enough front-row sable-and-station-wagon gals to go around, so this guy plucks one out of the front-row-center—chorus—I mean. She's probably a looker, but even the best of them can't trot their oomph around in the horse-show set and come up with the blue ribbons."

Joe left his chair and posed with arms outstretched like a traffic cop. "So here I am. St. Joseph South, protector against fortune hunters with one hand; gangsters with the other. At a price, of course."

Carton said lazily, "As we say in America, that's screwy." He gave Joe a thoughtful look. "I'm not questioning your version, Joey. I'm merely wondering about the job itself. I can't understand why a law firm—one as respectable as Van Pelt's, that is—should want to risk its reputation by hiring a detective with a suspended license to act as a bodyguard to one of its clients. I am assuming, of course, that your friend Van Pelt *does* have a reputation to risk."

Joe moved to the telephone. "You seem to forget that all three of us have worked for Van Pelt before. And when it comes to reputation he has more waxed up in his little mustache than the Bank of England. Why the suspicion?"

Carton shrugged. "Doing behind-the-scenes research for corporations and playing bodyguard in the open are hardly the same things. My suspicion is based solely on the opinion that Mr. Van Pelt seems scarcely the type who'd hire anyone to take care of a playboy client. The point being that every counselor with a license to practice prays nightly for a wealthy client endowed with the extraordinary faculty of getting into trouble. Deliberately taking steps to keep one out seems like lighting five-cent cigars with fifty-pound notes. In short, it's not like Van Pelt."

Joe picked up the telephone. "Sound logic, Kitch," he agreed. "Damned sound. But you're overlooking several important facts.

First, Van Pelt isn't just the kid's lawyer. He's one of the two trustees of the estate. Guarding the lad isn't his idea. That little inspiration comes from Parker Raleigh. Get that! *Mr. Parker Raleigh,* the guy's uncle!"

Carton whistled softly. The mention of Parker Raleigh to anyone who doesn't skip the financial pages was tantamount to quoting the cost of a naval program—or at least a couple of destroyers.

"Then that makes you the kid's new scoutmaster?"

"The same. Which brings me to point number two. He isn't a playboy in the usual sense. He's not exactly a playboy, and he's not wealthy. Not yet, he isn't. That's coming—the money, I mean—in a couple of months. If he marries he gets it right off. And that's what's got the relatives frothing at the mouth. They don't want their family crest kicked around by a dame who's not top drawer. Personally, I think it's because they're not enthusiastic about having a little oomph-and-hips gal becoming Mrs. Richard Raleigh and worming her heart into the family strong-box."

"Did Van Pelt tell you that?"

"Unh-unh! That's my idea. Van Pelt wasn't doing much telling. He's mainly worried about the Raleigh kid running around with thugs. He's afraid that one of these days he'll come floating down East River with baling wire where his tie ought to be."

"And what's he up to—running about with police characters?"

"Because of the terms of a will. Apparently his old man knew what he'd be like. Under the trust fund he gets just about enough to squeak along on until he's twenty-six. That's still a couple of months off. In the meantime he's been spending a lot more money than the trust allows—a hell of a lot more. So he gets involved in a racket that pays. That's what Van Pelt thinks anyway."

Joe gave the operator May's number. The voice that picked up the receiver sang, "Go-ud after-no-un. Gloucester-r-r Tow-e-r-r."

Joe mimicked the sing song greeting. "Apart-o-ment four— o-ny-un," and waited. There was no response. Then the operator said, "Miss Sands does not answer. Shall I leave a message?"

"Sure, sugar. Just tell her Mr. West called."

He hung up. His wrist said three-fifteen. He went to the closet and brought out a gray tweed reversible topcoat.

"I have an appointment with Parker Raleigh in fifteen minutes at Hillman Hospital. Wonder what the old buzzard's like." He examined the coat. The tweed side appeared cleaner and he slipped an arm into one of the sleeves. Kierney, who had been watching the weather from the bed, suddenly came to life.

"Hey, what you think you're doin'? That's my coat."

He reached for the coat, but Carton stopped him.

"Let him have it, James Michael, my boy," he advised. "You won't need it tonight. We're Mr. South's guests here until he decides to share the guineas. How about it, Joey?"

Joe's bark was several notes higher than normal.

"Goshdarnit, stop calling me Joey!" he shouted.

At the door he realized he was hatless and returned to the closet for a faded Homburg. Plastic features modeled into a mask of melancholy, he handed one of the hundred-dollar bills to the Englishman. Carton held the bill with the tips of his fingers as though it were a dead rat. Then, with a resigned gesture, he shrugged, folded it twice, and put it in his pocket. He said, " 'The jingle of the guinea helps the hurt that honour feels.' No sense thanking you for this, Joey. We'll both sweat a lot of blood working it out."

Joe slammed the door without replying.

━━━━━━━━━ *Chapter Two* ━━━━━━━━━

HE EMERGED into the street in a deluge of rain. Remembering traffic congestion on Broadway he hugged the building and ducked into the nearest subway station. Ten minutes later he was entering Hillman Hospital.

The hospital was situated on the lower West Side just before it becomes the Village. The group of several quiet, unassuming old buildings had once been a charitable institution. Traces of its humble origin were still visible in the discolored red brick and old-fashioned windows and doors. There the telltale marks ended. Inside it was as modern as Radio City.

During the war the wealthy philanthropist, Charles Gordon Hillman, had bought the site and the buildings and had it transformed into a hospital for the wealthy. One of the smaller buildings had been given over to charity patients and free clinics, but to occupy a private room in the main building meant that the patron could write a check in six figures at least.

To the right of the entrance hall was a large, glassed-in office. Behind the opening in a small window, a white-capped nurse busied herself with stacks of papers.

Joe approached the opening and asked for Parker Raleigh's room. She smiled coldly and said, "Oh, yes, Mr. South, I believe Mr. Raleigh is expecting you. His room is 315. One moment and I'll tell him you are here."

She turned her back as she did things to the switchboard. Joe glanced idly about the entrance hall. He had located the stairway immediately to the right of the elevators when the nurse returned

9

to the window. "Mr. Raleigh will see you in ten minutes," she informed him briefly and went back to her papers.

Joe walked toward the elevators directly across from the glass enclosure, watching the nurse from the corner of his eye. He was within three feet of the stairway when he saw her turn to the switchboard. The next moment he was climbing the stairs. He was slightly out of breath when he reached the third floor. Here the hospital held no slightest resemblance to the charitable refuge it had once been. On the contrary, there was little about it to suggest a hospital except lingering antiseptic odors and a soft-footed nurse moving down the corridor in front of him. Scarcely a sound reached him as he examined his surroundings.

The numbers over the doors told him that 315 was to his right. The door was open about two inches and he moved nearer to get a better view. The tableau presented by the occupants of the room stopped him for a moment. There was nothing unusual about it, but something in the atmosphere warned him that this was not just nurse and patient. There was more than ordinary professional concern in the face of the trim, dark-haired figure bending over the man on the bed. Joe couldn't see the man's face, but something in the nurse's eyes as she smiled at him reminded Joe of May on the few occasions she softened toward him. He didn't try to define the impression, but he was sure that if he were in Raleigh's shoes he'd try to make the most of the situation too. Maybe more than the most. Money doesn't buy that kind of nursing.

As he raised his hand to knock the girl looked up and saw him. She was almost as tall as Joe. Brunette and as streamlined as the interior of the building. Only *her* curves were in the right places, and she was as beautiful as a Red Cross poster. He knew by her slight flush that he had been right. She spoke softly to the man on the bed. "I assume this is the gentleman from Mr. Van Pelt's office." Her voice was cushioned and as smooth as velvet. Some nurse. He tried not to stare.

The patient turned his eyes slowly in Joe's direction. "Very well, Miss Gannon." He studied the detective for a moment and motioned him to enter. He didn't speak until Joe stood beside the bed. Then he said, "You're South?"

Joe nodded, and the sick man said, "I'm Parker Raleigh. Sit down. I'll be with you in a minute."

To the right of the door into the hall was a large clothes closet, its door partly open. From his position Joe noted two suits hanging on a rack. He wondered what a man lying sick in a hospital bed could possibly want with a complete wardrobe.

Joe's eyes traveled from the wardrobe to the man on the bed. It wasn't hard to see that he was unaccustomed to enforced idleness. He made even that undersized bed look as if it had been designed for the chairman of the board. The investment represented in the richly brocaded dressing gown he was wearing would have kept the detective for a week, including Scotches and sodas. The slippers beside the bed were well-worn, but even Joe knew they hadn't come from Gimbel's basement. His hair was the kind of gray smart women try to acquire at forty. Joe thought he might be in the middle fifties.

"All right, South," Raleigh's voice broke into Joe's musing. It sounded like the right side of Hyde Park. "Let's get down to business. Mr. Van Pelt tells me you've done jobs for him before."

Joe nodded. "Sure. Mr. Van Pelt and I understand each other."

Raleigh didn't smile. He said, "Then, of course, you know what your job is." He paused and stared speculatively at Joe. "I sent for you because I'm not in the habit of hiring men I can't judge for myself. Stuyvesant Van Pelt's opinion goes a long way, of course, and I hope he isn't mistaken this time."

"Mr. Van Pelt isn't taking chances where I'm concerned, Mr. Raleigh. He doesn't make mistakes. He can't afford to."

The older man glanced at him sharply and frowned. "All right, South. Suppose you give *me* some facts about yourself."

"Oh, sure," Joe agreed. "Where do I begin? I'm thirty-five and white. I'd have graduated from the university where I was studying law if I'd been able to control the impulse to poke a swell-head professor. That did it and I'm still trying not to lose control. Then I tried the police force in a certain city and quit because I couldn't stand the routine and dirty politics. I'm single for the same reason. Since then I've free-lanced in New York, Atlantic City, Palm Beach, Miami and every banana port south of the Canal. I'm as honest as my profession allows and I've donated myself a sheepskin for never having been caught on the wrong side of the law."

"That's enough for the moment, South. Your independence does you credit." Raleigh settled back against the pillows. "Now. Just what did Mr. Van Pelt tell you?"

Joe didn't like that. He hadn't come here to give information but to get it. He would have to play along for the moment, however. He said, "He tells me you are a bachelor with a niece and a nephew. Your nephew, Richard, has recently been playing cops and robbers with a couple of mugs—identity unknown—who are apt to rub his nose in the mud. Your niece, Naomi, it seems, got wind of his pranks and came through, bold like, with a message to Garcia. Right?"

Raleigh nodded. His eyes were cold. He said through stiff lips, "Right." The sick man wasn't liking this at all.

11

"When he got that far," Joe continued, "naturally I wanted to know what a wealthy young Fauntleroy was doing messing around with that kind of society. Van Pelt explained what appeared to be your niece's idea. Namely, that he'd got himself mixed up in some kind of racket with them. It seems she suspected something was wrong when he began to spend more money than his allowance provided. Much more money."

Joe struck a match and lit a cigarette from a crumpled package. He passed the package to Raleigh. The older man waved it aside impatiently. "Is that all?" he asked.

"All," Joe told him, "except that my job would last until Richard's twenty-sixth birthday. In other words, until January 30—two months from today."

He was watching Raleigh through a cloud of smoke. Suddenly Joe was convinced that something was being held back. It made him uneasy. He said, "Of course, Mr. Raleigh, I naturally assumed that a man in your position would have investigated the situation a little further before taking a hysterical girl's word." He paused to let that sink in, and added evenly, "What did you find?"

Raleigh's face didn't change. He said, "That's my business, South. You're hired for one thing—to keep my nephew out of trouble. My family's affairs don't concern you. . . ."

Joe didn't wait for more. He almost knocked the chair over as he bounced to his feet. His face was flushed; his eyes steely. He stood over the arrogant figure on the bed. He said in a voice that rasped, "You're darned well right they don't concern me. What do you think I am? A whining busybody to pick your private skeletons clean and throw the morsels over back fences? Take your darned job and your whimpering brat and to hell with both of them! The sooner they got there the better!"

He turned without waiting for an answer and stormed toward the door. Raleigh's voice stopped him as his hand touched the knob.

"That attitude won't get you anywhere, South. Come back and cool off."

Joe looked at Raleigh suspiciously. A half-smile lifted the corners of the sick man's mouth. That did it. Joe relaxed, but his anger was still bubbling. He stood over the bed and said between tight lips, "Okay, it's your move."

Raleigh's smile was all the way now. "Quite a temper you have there."

"Not temper," Joe corrected. "Pride. You're no different from all the other guys that shuffle gold and clip coupons. You have no control over your families and when one of them gets in trouble your only concern is how to keep your gilt-edge names out of the headlines. I repeat. Don't hand me any of that stuff about prying. I don't give a hang about your private affairs except that the more facts I have the better I can do my job."

"Be that as it may, South," Raleigh snapped, "I can usually take care of my own."

Joe had planted himself gingerly in the white chair again. He grunted, "It don't look much like it in this case."

Raleigh was still smiling. He said, "Right. I can guess now why your license was suspended. You ought to try to control that temper."

Joe said, "So you know that, do you? Van Pelt didn't miss a trick when you talked to him. Skip it, and let's get this over with."

"My idea exactly, South," he frowned. "You can understand all this is extremely distasteful to me."

It was a concession to apology. Joe said, "Van Pelt mentioned your nephew's allowance as part of the root of the trouble. Why is it so small against the amount of the inheritance?"

Raleigh leaned forward. "All right, South. You can have it for what it's worth. My brother, the children's father, left a fortune in trust for them. They were young—motherless—and he made me their guardian as well as one of the trustees." He paused and looked at Joe as if uncertain how much he should tell the detective. After a moment he went on. "The will is a complicated one, the kind a man of my brother's temperament would be likely to make. Richard's income is only two thousand a year until his twenty-sixth birthday— two months from today. If he marries before that he inherits immediately."

"Yeah. Van Pelt told me all that. What was the idea tying the girl's dough in knots?"

Raleigh stiffened. "That has nothing to do with your job, South. We'll stick to the pertinent facts."

"Okay. Only it's still screwy. She gets the same allowance until she marries. Then her only reward is a substantial increase, and she still has to wait five years for her share of the estate. If she doesn't marry she has to wait till she's thirty for the 'substantial' increase." He shrugged. "But I haven't ever been a wealthy parent —thank God—so I don't need any pointers. Skip it."

Raleigh's smile was sardonic. "I haven't either, South, so we'll both skip it. It isn't as bad as you think," he added. "After all, Naomi is nearly twenty-five, and the will protects her in case anything happens to me or to Richard."

"I see," Joe mused. "Van Pelt tells me that Richard has been up to these tricks for over a year now. It isn't hard to guess that he got impatient and decided to grab himself some dough the easy way." Something about the set look in Raleigh's eyes prompted him to add, "He hasn't had advances against his inheritance, has he?"

Raleigh glared, "Look here, South. Need you be so darned inquisitive?"

Joe flushed and started to rise. Raleigh waved him back. "All right, all right," he said testily. "We'll never get anywhere if you don't control that temper."

"And we'll never get anywhere if you don't try to remember that I need information if I'm to work intelligently," Joe retorted.

Raleigh said with evident distaste, "Naomi thinks he's had well over fifty thousand dollars from Van Pelt during the last two years. I learned this only recently. I pay his debts, within reason, of course, but I've refused to allow him more than the amount provided by the trust." He closed his lips with a snap.

Joe said, "That's better. It brings us to the question as to whether he's messing around with gangsters for profit or just for excitement. In other words, if he had his legacy now, would he drop them?"

"What do you mean?"

"If what Van Pelt says is true I'm afraid the gentlemen Richard is tangled with won't be so easy to brush off."

Raleigh looked worried. He said, "Um-m. Yes. I see what you mean. But"—the coldness crept back into his voice—"it's your job now. Take it or leave it. I usually pay for what I get and I expect results."

In spite of the arrogance Raleigh's voice was tired. For a few minutes Joe had actively disliked him until he remembered that he wasn't a well man. Illness had wiped some of the steel from the handsome features and Joe suddenly felt sorry for him. He said, "And I take it I'm to find the root of the trouble and nip it or see that Richard doesn't get clipped?"

"That's exactly, South." Raleigh relaxed against the pillows. For a moment he actually looked embarrassed. "And there's another thing. Er ... ah ... I'd rather Richard wouldn't know that I've ... ah ... hired a bodyguard for him. I'm sure you will get better results that way."

Joe hid a smile. The Raleigh pride must be protected. He said with a straight face, "Will he think I'm a Russian prince or just a long-lost cousin?"

The smile that crossed Raleigh's mouth this time was attractive. He said, "This must sound like a penny thriller to you, South. No, I merely told him that I was expecting an old friend from Montana You needn't bother about the town. Dick has never been west of Philadelphia."

Joe said, "Okay," and waited. This ought to be good.

"You'll have to stay at the house, of course," Raleigh reached for the dressing gown and took out a bunch of keys. "There's the key to the place on 78th Street. You should find Dick there sooner or later. Naomi is staying at a friend's apartment in Gramercy Park."

Joe took the key and scribbled the house number on a scrap of paper. He said, "Okay. Anyone else I'll have to cope with out there?"

"Only the maid. The other servants are on holiday until I get out of here."

Joe said, "I'll keep you posted." Raleigh didn't answer. At the door Joe looked back. The patient's eyes were already closed.

The subway back to the hotel was crowded. Those suits in Raleigh's closet and the nurse. Did the nurse come with the room or the room with the nurse? And who did you have to be to get a nurse like that? A sign on a platform said Times Square.

The Hotel Brant loomed through the weather like a gray ghost Carton and Kierney were no longer there. The suitcase hadn't been completely unpacked and it took only a few minutes to finish the job. He added a respectable camel hair topcoat, some clean shirts socks and the half empty pint of rye Kierney had deserted. He didn't remove the neat .32 under the pile of shirts at the bottom of the suitcase. There wasn't anything in the closet that looked like Montana. The Homburg he was wearing wouldn't have passed for a half-gallon hat in Hoboken. He did it the easy way. On a shelf in the closet was a walking stick Carton had affected when he first came to New York. Joe took it. He looked around to be sure he hadn't forgotten anything. Then he called Pete. As he swung through the street door the rain-washed cab skidded to a stop at the curb. Joe made a dash for it and climbed in.

Pete said, "Lousy weather we're havin', ain't it?"

Joe grinned and gave him the 78th Street address.

The Raleigh residence was typical of others in the immediate neighborhood. Built when quality of workmanship meant something, and Dutch conservatism still exercised its influence with moneyed New Yorkers, the house stood with quiet dignity in the shadow of streamlined apartment buildings to the right and left.

Pete looked at the hundred-dollar bill in Joe's hand.

"Aw, Joey. I told you I couldn't change that. Who d'ya think I'm workin' for? Brink . . ." Joe silenced him with a lifted hand. He said,

"Don't worry, Pete. I'll have the change later on. Stick around somewhere. I might need you this evening."

The button Joe pressed emitted low, musical chimes. Light footsteps approached. Through the translucent glass the figure looked trim and neat.

"Not bad, maybe," Joe mused.

The girl who opened the door was as black as Joe's Homburg. Her figure was not as inviting as Gannon's. Joe said, "Holy cripes!"

She said, "Peace, it's wonderful!" and grinned widely, showing glistening teeth. One of Father Divine's educated converts. He followed the neatly clad maid through the foyer into a spacious, beautifully appointed room.

"That fire'll be fine to get some of the rain out of me, but I need a drink, too. How about it?"

She grinned, took the reversible, hat and stick and hung them in a closet. She returned a few minutes later with a syphon of seltzer, whisky in a cut-glass decanter and a small silver dish of ice cubes, which she put down on a table.

"My name is Precious Lamb," she informed him. There was no trace of Dixie in her voice. She probably had never been south of Newark. "Just pull the cord when you want to go to your room."

Joe was pouring whisky into the glass. At the door she turned and said to his back, "Peace! It's wonderful." He swung around, but she was gone. He added ice to his glass and addressed the door. "Not from you, sister. Not from you."

Chapter Three

JOE SLUMPED into a wing chair in front of the fire and pushed a footstool into position. All the comforts of home. Somebody else's home. Three hundred and fifty dollars a month for sitting around in front of a fireplace drinking somebody else's liquor. Somebody else's maid to wait on you. To hell with Communism.

He took a sip from his glass and surveyed the room. In one corner was a Chickering grand piano. He picked up his drink and fingered the keys. In the middle of *Dinah* a telephone rang in the room across the hall. When the bell continued to ring he followed the sound and picked up the receiver. The voice that came over the wire was high and arrogant. Joe explained his presence.

"Oh yes." It was Richard Raleigh. "Uncle Park said you'd be getting in this afternoon. I'm anxious to meet you." Joe thought the voice was mocking. "Have you had dinner?"

When Joe answered in the negative, Richard said, "Why don't you come down and join us? We're at the Timbuctoo. You'll be in time for a round of cocktails. The Timbuctoo is on 52nd Street between Sixth and Seventh."

Joe agreed and hung up. He was startled by a small sound and turned to find Precious Lamb in the doorway dressed for the street.

"This is my night off," she told him. "I think I'd better show you

16

to your room before I leave." She picked up his bag and he followed her upstairs. She opened a door into a pleasantly proportioned bedroom facing the rear of the house.

She busied herself arranging his things in a highboy. When she had finished she moved toward the door.

"I think you'll find everything you need for tonight. I'll be back early to get your breakfast."

Joe said, "Peace! It's wonderful."

She grinned and went without comment.

Whoever had given the Timbuctoo its name had chosen it for euphony. Joe couldn't see any other reason. There was little to distinguish it from other night clubs in the vicinity.

Richard Raleigh was seated in a far corner and as Joe approached he rose. Opposite him was a girl who was all eyes and mouth. Raleigh said, "You're Mr. South, aren't you? I'm Raleigh." They shook hands. "And this is Miss Evans," Raleigh added.

The girl acknowledged the introduction with a giggle. She wore long straight black hair in a braid over her head. On closer inspection she had more than just eyes and mouth to recommend her. So this must be the little "momma and poppa" gal the guy was trying to horse up with. She had things all right—maybe not the kind it takes to get a bid to a brass-hat frolic—not by the front door, anyway—but things.

Richard Raleigh waited for Joe to be seated. He was about five-feet-eleven and well built. His hair had begun to thin back over an onion-shaped forehead that made him look several years older than his twenty-six years. A wispy mustache partially concealed a weak mouth. There was nothing about him to suggest kinship with Parker Raleigh. The waiter pulled up a chair for Joe and they sat down.

The Evans girl studied him over the rim of her glass. She raised it as she caught his eye and smiled through the liquid. She rested her cheek on a palm and inspected him with appraisal. She said, "Let me think. Who do you remind me of? Um-m . . . Oh, I have it. Jack Oakie. That's who you look like. Jack Oakie."

Joe grinned uncomfortably.

The ends of Raleigh's mustache came up in what was meant for a smile.

"That's the first time I've known Milly to be right. She's always telling people they look like someone on the screen. However, you do remind me of that clown."

Joe didn't like the tone of the last remark. In fact, he didn't think he was going to like Richard Raleigh. Raleigh changed the subject.

"Uncle Park tells me that you and he did some work together out in Montana. I'm sure he's glad to return some of the hospitality you

17

showed him. Too bad you found him laid up."

He took out a fountain pen and scribbled on a pad and handed the pad and pen across to Joe.

"We've been drinking daiquiris," he said. "You write your own ticket."

The pad said "Table 42." Underneath in Dick's scrawl was written "2 daiquiris." Joe added "1 double Scotch and soda." Raleigh crooked a finger at a waiter and gave him the pad. The floor by this time was crowded with dancing couples. A red-haired girl in a stainless steel evening gown and slippers was dancing with a man twelve inches shorter than she. Everything about him said "coats and suits." He appeared to be having a good time and looked sober. When they turned the girl nodded to Joe. She was one of the most striking redheads he had ever seen. Something vaguely familiar stirred Joe's memory. He managed to catch himself in time to ignore the greeting.

Richard had also seen the girl's gesture. He smiled and leaned forward. Elbows on the table, chin on clasped hands he watched Joe. He said, "What do you think of New York weather? Kind of takes the wild out of the woolly West, doesn't it?"

Joe played with the fountain pen. He didn't like the way young Raleigh was studying him.

"Not particularly. This is the kind of weather we look forward to back home. It's the kind we hope for on our vacations. You'll probably not believe me, but back in Montana I'm awakened every morning at six by an earthquake."

Milly giggled. She was good at it. "Oh, Mr. South, you're a scream."

The waiter came with the drinks. The quality of the Scotch wasn't bad. Joe had no complaint to make about the quantity. The Timbuctoo did right by its patrons.

Richard rose. So did the ends of the mustache. Joe decided the mustache was like a trained seal.

"Will you two please excuse me? I see some friends I'd like to speak to."

Milly leaned forward and put her hand on Joe's sleeve, looking at Dick.

"Don't stay long, Dick. I'm afraid to be alone with these strong, silent men from the West."

"So I see," was all he said, as he moved through the crowd on the dance floor to a table in the far corner where two men were sipping coffee. They hadn't been there when Joe came in. Both were in evening clothes.

One was fat. So fat he had trouble reaching the table with his elbows. What hair he had appeared to rest on his shoulders. There was almost no neck. Blonde, almost albino brows hovered over colorless eyes. His fat sensuous lips drooled over a well-chewed cigar.

The other, in comparison, was well built. His shining black hair waved in a perfect marcel and his mustache was waxed and pointed. Joe caught his eye across the room suddenly and was startled at the intensity of the man's stare. Neither of the men rose as Richard joined them. His presence was taken for granted.

Joe and Milly finished their drinks. Then they drank Richard's. He saw that she was beginning to feel the effects of the cocktails. She watched him under sultry lids. There was no giggle this time.

"You know, Mr. South, I could go for you in a big way."

"Most of them do," he answered idly. He was wondering how much she knew about Richard's business. He decided to find out. He said, "We'd better watch our step though. Dick's got some tough friends."

"Afraid?" she pouted.

"Not afraid—only careful." He motioned toward Dick who was still at the table with the two men. "He might get tough. Looks like he has some pretty hefty playmates."

The pout left the girl's lips and for a moment a frightened look showed in her eyes. Then she shrugged.

"Oh, them. They may get by with telling Dicky when to change his diapers but they can't kick me around. Me and Dicky understand each other." She pressed her lips together and an angry light chased fear from her eyes. "Dicky's smarter than they are. Just wait till . . ." She clapped her hand over her mouth suddenly and gave a small gasp. "What am I talking about? Come on. Let's dance."

"All right," Joe agreed. He knew he wouldn't get any more out of her now. "But no jitterbug stuff."

Young Raleigh's back was to them as they edged onto the floor. Joe put his arm around her waist. Her bare back felt warm and sleek under his touch. Brushing stray hairs from his cheek he whispered into her ear, "Just call me Joey."

The floor was jammed. Milly was taller than she looked when seated.

She slid up on her toes, clinging to him with a sinuous sway of her hips. Her firm, slender body snuggled softly to his and he felt the rise and fall of pulsing breasts as she followed him expertly. Boy, young Raleigh knew how to pick them.

The man with the mustache was following him with hot, intense eyes. Presently Richard turned. Joe knew there was suspicion in his glance. He pretended not to notice. The music stopped and Milly still clung to him. He released her hold gently. She was definitely intoxicated. So it wasn't altogether his personality that had made her so warmly responsive. They returned to the table, Joe steadying

19

her into her chair. He said, "Excuse me. I just remembered a call I should have made the minute I got off the train."

The girl's giggle was alcoholic.

"Oh, Mr. South, you're so funny. It's the second door to the left."

Joe cut his way around the tables of the smoke-filled room. A small, gypsy-faced girl in tweeds was standing near the door leading to the canopied check-counter. He thought for a moment she was going to speak to him, but as he passed on she turned to the youth behind her. He didn't recall having met her and he didn't have time to find out now.

The blonde hatcheck was busy in the back. Before she had time to turn he had selected an umbrella from a stand across the counter and was out on 52nd Street. Raising the umbrella he tacked into the wind toward a drug store a half block east.

Inside the telephone booth he dialed three different numbers. None of them answered. Then he called his room at the hotel. Kierney answered. Quickly Joe explained where he was and described the two men with Richard Raleigh. Kierney's low whistle was excited. He was serious when he spoke.

"Listen, Joey, if the guy with the mustache has a cut under it, and if he's a little gimpy, and if he's with a Poland China that looks like he's ready for the smokehouse, and if you seen 'em both at the Timbuctoo, you got yourself into some extra elegant company." The Irishman paused for breath, and speaking softly and distinctly continued, "The guy with the mustache is Frankie Shasta and the chowderhead is Porky Wiener. Only don't call him Porky to his face."

Joe said, "Thanks," sarcastically.

"That's all right," Kierney replied generously. "Call on me any time, Joey. I don't know what you're gettin' into, but me and Kitch is glad we ain't in it."

A girl in a greenish yellow slicker blocked his way as he opened the door of the booth. She came just to Joe's shoulder. He recognized her immediately as the girl who had almost spoken to him as he left the night club. The tweeds were covered now by the slicker, but he remembered the brown hat and the wet green feather. He started to pass her, but she put out a hand and stopped him.

"You're Mr. South, aren't you?" she greeted him. "I'm Naomi Raleigh. I talked with Uncle Park right after you left the hospital this afternoon." She had hardly paused for breath. "I tried to catch you at the house, but you had already gone. I stopped at the Timbuctoo where I knew I'd find Dick and saw you at his table."

Joe said nothing. He had suddenly recognized her voice. It was the one he had heard coming from Van Pelt's office that morning.

He was as fascinated by the gamin-like animation of her features as he had been by her brother's mustache. She paused at last and gave him an appraising stare. After a moment she observed, "You don't look like a detective."

"That's what they all say," he retorted disgustedly as he drew out a chair for her. He sat down. "Or else they tell me I'm the very image of some guy that hangs around Hollywood."

She ignored the chair and turned back toward the street door.

"Please let's not be childish," she begged. "I came here to talk with you about Dick. Charles is with me and if you'll wait a moment I'll get him. I won't keep you long."

The detective nodded and drew out a cigarette. The difference between Richard and Naomi was more than just a toss up. Under the hat was a mind. One of those high-nosed Eastern finishing schools had dusted it up, but she'd started out with plenty and still had it. He shrugged. It meant more trouble. The Raleighs, like the mumps, hit all points at once.

The girl returned almost immediately trailed by a wispy young man without hat or topcoat. He was taller than Naomi by about an inch. His walk was slightly swivel-hipped. Several pencils protruded from the breast pocket of a tweed sports jacket.

Naomi introduced them. His name was Charles Emmett Shermond. From the way she pronounced it Joe thought he was supposed to recognize it. He didn't. Shermond extended a limp hand that felt like a fistful of putty. His voice had about the same quality. "I'm happy to meet you, Mr. South," he murmured, but didn't look it.

The girl removed her hat. She said without preliminary, "Dick is with that girl again, isn't he, Mr. South?"

Apparently her uncle had brought her up to date. Joe extracted a toothpick from the fly-specked glass at his elbow and broke it into bits. His resentment increased. He said. "You picked a swell night to go gallivanting around watching your brother. I thought I'd fallen heir to that job."

Naomi leaned toward him and smiled.

"Now look, Mr. South . . . No. I expect I'd better call you Joe. We're going to be together a lot." Joe shuddered. The anything that might have happened was beginning to. He pictured himself trying to tail a couple of mugs with this gypsy girl-scout on his heels. She hadn't paused for breath. "Joe, you're not listening to me. Don't you think I'm capable of taking care of myself? That's the trouble with Dick and Uncle Park. They think I'm still a school kid. I know it would be thrilling to help you with Dick."

Joe was rude. He said, "Skip the melodrama, sister. You've been reading the tabloids."

His glance traveled to Charles and he wondered what the attraction was.

He wasn't aware that he hadn't been listening until she said, "Why don't you pay some attention to me, Joe? I just said Charles and I are going back to the Timbuctoo with you."

Charles was nervously toying with the pencils in his pocket. His remonstration was weak.

"Darling, I think you're overdoing this. I've told you before. Time will take care of it. Time cures everything." He appealed to Joe. "Don't you believe in Time, Mr. South?"

"Yeah, Mr. Shermond is right. Time. Your Time is my Time. Good old Time. Time Marches On." Joe humored the boy. Naomi's smile was elfin. She was enjoying Joe's levity.

Enthusiasm came into Charles' eyes. He offered the putty again. His voice was precise and dry. "Mr. South, you make me very happy. I didn't expect to find you sympathetic. It goes to prove that the true understanding of Time has a leavening effect."

"You see," Shermond said to Naomi. "Mr. South will handle the whole thing. It's his job. Certainly you don't wish to go to that awful place again."

Joe watched Shermond with renewed interest. There was going to be fun in this after all. He said, "What the hell! It's okay with me if you go back. Do you suppose it will be all right with your brother?"

Naomi shrugged.

"Oh, Dick won't make a scene. If that's what you mean. He hates scenes." She grinned impishly. "I'm the one who likes them."

Watching the rising excitement in her eyes Joe could believe it. This was going to be difficult. He'd probably never get rid of the brat now. He put a hand on her wrist.

"Wait," he cautioned. "We've got to make this look straight. What will your brother think if he sees us come in together?"

That stopped her, but only for a second. She patted Joe's hand.

"You're right, Joey. You go ahead and Charles and I will follow."

Joe groaned. On top of everything else she'd started that. What was it about him that made everybody call him Joey two minutes after they'd met him? As he entered the club the blonde hatcheck nodded to the orchestra leader. The band swung into *Montana Moon*. The music followed him to the table and ended with a crash of cymbals and bass drum as he sat down.

Now who the hell had done that? It was his evening for bad breaks. There was a round of applause. A few curious eyes swept his table. Milly was still alone, drowsily resting one cheek on her hand. An untouched daiquiri was at her elbow. Joe drank it and she sat up.

Shermond and Naomi were elbowing their way toward the table

Smoke swirled overhead like heavy mist. Naomi smiled at Milly, who merely glowered sulkily. Joe said, "Do you know these people, Milly?"

Milly got up shakily. "Sure. Little sister Naomi and her lap dog," and moved unsteadily away, holding on to the backs of chairs for support. Naomi's smile was innocent.

"I don't think Dick's fiancée likes me very well."

Joe raised an eyebrow. "So she's the one."

Naomi was shedding the slicker. Her lips came down in a grimace. "Oh yes. Didn't you know? It's part of the pressure he's putting on Uncle Park . . . and me," she added under her breath.

They sat down. Joe eyed Naomi thoughtfully. "When is this to be?"

Naomi shrugged. "Oh, he's been threatening to do it for the last six months. It's just another of his wild ideas. She's probably his 'secret weapon.' "

Joe was angry again. Parker Raleigh hadn't bothered to mention that small item. Small hell! Just an example of his expert side-stepping. No telling how much more he'd skipped. He shrugged. Good thing Van Pelt had hinted at it. He scowled and said, "How about a little drink?"

Naomi grinned. "A very good idea."

Shermond looked at her reproachfully.

"Please, dear, why do you come to these dreadful places?" He turned sharply as he felt a hand on his shoulder. It was Richard Raleigh.

"Why the hurry, Charles, my boy?" He lurched and brought the ends of his mustache up for Naomi's benefit. She half rose from her chair. Richard waved her back and looked at Joe. "Did Milly introduce you folks?"

Joe said, "In her own sweet way."

Dick slid into a chair and looked around stupidly.

"Where the hell did she get to?" he growled.

Naomi shrugged and motioned across the room.

"Looks like your future helpmeet found more desirable company. More of them anyway."

Joe had seen her at the same time. She was holding on to the back of the chair Dick had occupied at Shasta's table. The dapper Italian had risen and appeared to be arguing with her. He had her by the arm. Dick got up and said angrily, "By heaven, I'll break that greasy Dago's neck!"

Naomi started to protest, but at that moment Milly jerked away from Shasta and started drunkenly across the crowded floor. Dick met her halfway and led her back to his table. She didn't sit down. She was watching Joe under her sultry lids. The girl turned toward him slowly, still staring. Suddenly, before any of them realized what was happening, she flung the cocktail she had picked up into Joe's face. It was followed by an ashtray which missed. She did better with Richard's fountain pen. It caught him squarely in the mouth. Ink splashed his shirt front. For the second time that day pens had been used as missiles. This time the ink was green.

Richard acted fast. He had Milly's arm behind her. She struggled and shrieked, "He's a gol darned lousy detective!"

Joe got up wiping his face with his napkin. The crowd stopped swaying and the band struck up a louder note. Dick said, "Let's get out of here quick."

Joe was speechless. He knew his identity had been exposed somewhere along the line, but he hadn't been prepared for anything like this. He picked up the fountain pen and dabbed at the ink with his napkin. He drank Shermond's drink, then Naomi's. His voice when he spoke to Naomi was hoarse. "Your little brother's suggestion was pretty good. Let's get going."

Shermond had disappeared in search of his car. Raleigh had ordered his sent over from a parking lot. Milly was ominously quiet. Cooking up more trouble, Joe thought. He decided to take a hand. The situation needed a little ironing out. He moved closer to Dick.

"I don't know what this is all about." He nodded toward Milly. "I have no intention of getting mixed up with family squabbles. I think I'd better clear out and spend the night at a hotel."

It was a good try and Raleigh followed through.

"Take it easy, South. Don't let a little disturbance upset you. Naomi and I have had a disagreement, but then we always disagree. As for Milly, I should have known better. Three drinks and she accuses LaGuardia of being on Mussolini's pay roll."

Milly jerked away from Dick, "It wasn't my idea," she spat. "One of your . . ." Dick slapped a hand over her mouth.

He said, "Keep your sweet little trap shut, darling." His lips were smiling, but under the green light his eyes were dangerous.

Joe grinned. It was all clear now. He grunted as Dick took his hand away from Milly's mouth and turned to him.

"Let's get out of this, South. Maybe we can get straightened out in a quieter place." He looked at Naomi. "What about it, kid?"

Naomi's smile reminded Joe of the cat with yellow feathers on its whiskers. She said, "Anything you say, Dicky."

With Milly between Joe and Richard they drove North on Lexington in Raleigh's coupê. Shermond followed in his shabby sedan with Naomi. Milly had apparently forgotten her resentment. Joe accepted the insistent pressure of her knee as a bid for amity. He was perfectly willing to forget it.

A block from the Harlem River they stopped in front of a small café. The metal sign swaying in the rain announced that Rupperts could be had there. Shermond's car drew up behind.

The bartender, a fat Syrian with a dirty apron shielding his paunch, nodded to Dick as they took their seats. His little pig eyes were watchful. The only other occupants of the room, a man who looked like a Portuguese and a skinny negress, were drunk. Their voices rose shrilly.

Dick turned to South.

"You *are* a detective, aren't you?"

Joe lighted a cigarette and blew smoke into Shermond's eyes. He said, "You work fast, Raleigh. How about a ham sandwich?"

Dick signaled the bartender. Then he said impatiently, "Don't try to kid me, South. You left the club to investigate my friends, didn't you?"

The detective shouted to the bartender, "Put some mustard on it." Then to Richard, "Friends?"

Richard grunted.

"This is all so damned silly. You'd think I was a one-year-old. Naomi, is this your idea or Uncle Park's?"

Naomi's eyes were mischievous. She reached over and touched his hand.

"Darling, it was part mine and part Uncle's. If you hadn't insisted on not letting me in on the fun I'd never have gone to Uncle Park."

Dick's mouth was tight. He snapped.

"You little fool. Why can't you leave me alone? Fun! Nuts on that! You don't know what you're talking about!"

"Oh yes I do." Naomi put her elbows on the table and cupped her chin in her hands. Joe thought she looked like one of those angel-faced choir boys who fill the roto sections at Christmas and Easter. He was sure now that her innocent tale-bearing had not been entirely responsible for Van Pelt's and the older Raleigh's interest in this business.

Milly, who had been silent since they entered the tavern, stared at Naomi malignantly and snarled, "I hate your guts, Naomi Raleigh. But take my advice and let Dicky paddle his own canoe. It won't get you anywhere to butt in."

Dick scowled. "Didn't I tell you to keep those beautiful lips closed, darling? They look and sound a lot better in that position."

Naomi became serious. "Look, Dick. I really was teasing you, but Uncle Park is worried. I came looking for you tonight to beg you to stop going on like this until he's out of the hospital. If he hadn't been worried he'd never have sent Mr. South to you."

Dick said, "For heaven's sake, don't go melodramatic on me. I want to get this straight. Just what do you mean, go on like this?"

Joe decided this was his cue. He took a bite out of the ham sandwich and pointed a slice of dill pickle at Richard.

"I'll tell you what you're doing. You *are* acting like a one-year-old. Now I have no objection to your acting that way. You can be a dope if you want to. I've done about everything else and a job's a job. If I don't like changing your diapers at least I'm getting paid for it. You can run around with second-rate ex-torpedoes like Shasta and Wiener if you want to. Only get this straight"—he shook the pickle in Dick's face for emphasis—"keep off the front page and out of the morgue. At least until after January 30. Then you can come over to my apartment and borrow my gun. I'll let you blow your stupid brains out and I won't even look up from the funny papers."

It was the longest speech he'd made that night. He ended by snapping two inches off the pickle. If he had expected Raleigh to be angry he was disappointed. He had the mustache under control. For the first time Naomi looked at the detective without sympathy. She said angrily, "That's about the poorest psychology I ever heard. Uncle Park must have had a relapse when he hired you."

It was all on the table now. There were no more references to Montana. Joe had known since before leaving the Timbuctoo that Raleigh was wise to him. This time there was affection in Naomi's eyes as she touched Dick's hand.

"Never mind, Dick. You know your business better than Joe South does. Only, darling, promise me you'll be careful."

Dick didn't answer. He gazed moodily at Milly. Naomi pressed his fingers. "Promise," she insisted.

Dick responded suddenly. He put his other hand over hers. He was still slightly drunk but his eyes were moody.

"All right," he growled. "All you want is a promise to be careful. I don't know why. I hereby promise to be careful in all things. In crossing crossings cautiously; in not crossing platinum blondes; in not crossing business associates because my sister doesn't like them. Okay, kid, I promise." He smiled at her. "And now we've had enough gloom for one night. I'll buy you a drink. In fact, I'll buy everybody a drink."

Joe nodded over the last crust of his sandwich. The mood of the party changed.

Naomi's eyes brightened. She even winked at Joe. "Now we can have fun," she announced and looked at Milly. "Come on," she pleaded. "Don't be a stick. What will you have, Milly?"

Milly's smile was forced, but Joe gave her due credit. She said, "All right, Lady Astor. I can be as good a sport as you. I'll have a daiquiri for a change."

Dick said, "Atta girl! We'll make it a celebration. Come on, South, you can drink a toast to mine and Milly's engagement at the same time."

Naomi said, "Are you going to start that again, Dick?"

"Start it!" Richard scowled into his drink and put a hand over Milly's. "We're going to finish it tomorrow. How do you like *that?*" He wavered against Naomi and put his face close to hers. "No more strings, eh, sis? No more lectures from Uncle Park and Stuyvie. I'll show that Dutch uncle a thing or two. I've got more strings on my racket than Bill Tilden." He straightened up and smiled at Milly. "This time tomorrow night I'll have the license in my pocket, and by next week you'll be Mrs. Richard Lyons Raleigh. How about it, mush-face?"

Milly was pouting. She giggled, "Dicky, I thought you said it was a secret." But she was obviously pleased.

"Secret, hell! I'm tired of asking somebody every time I have to change my shorts. They didn't think I'd do it. I'll show 'em."

Joe said, "Hadn't you better have another drink and call it a night, Raleigh?" He grinned. "Drink twice before you speak. Them's my motto. Then you can't speak."

Shermond looked pained all over again. He was trying not to look at Joe and Raleigh.

"Naomi, darling," his voice was pleading. "I can't stand much more of this. Must we stay?"

Naomi bent forward and stroked his chin.

"All right, precious. Just one little drink and we'll go. Just for me? Please?"

Shermond shrugged without answering and looked at the greasy-paunched bartender with distaste. Joe ordered a Scotch and soda. The others ordered daiquiries. Shermond still refused.

The detective relaxed and smiled in response to Naomi's wink. She was as good at it as Milly was with the giggles. Maybe she'd be fun if he didn't have this job on his hands. She'd bundle up into just about the right kind of package to tote around town the next time May got into one of her all-too-frequent independent moods. He shook his head to clear it. He was beginning to feel groggy and tired, and the close atmosphere of the dingy tavern was giving him a headache.

Naomi rose and pulled on the slicker. Shermond got up eagerly.

"Not going to leave us?" Richard's voice was mocking.

Naomi answered for Shermond. "You know how Charles is, Dick," she reminded him. "He doesn't drink and he's a working man. It's getting late," she added, and to Joe, "Keep the home fires burning, Father Brown."

Joe went to the door with them and heard the car start. He

glanced at his watch. It was ten minutes past twelve. They had been in the place much longer than he had thought. He wondered if Shermond would take Naomi back to the Raleigh house now that she and Dick appeared to have made up.

He returned to the table and picked up his drink. It would be the last for the evening. Dick and Milly were dancing again. Joe lifted his glass to the couple and swallowed its contents in one gulp. What a job this had turned out to be. Well, he had been paid in advance. If the job ended tomorrow he would still be ahead. He would see Parker Raleigh in the morning and tell him how the plan had backfired before it had time to get a good start.

He sat still with his elbows resting on the table and his chin in his hands. Richard and Milly, swaying to the rhythm of the music, merged into one. Then there were two couples. Two Richards and two Millies and two juke boxes. The door came up at a forty-five-degree angle, but the couple danced on. Suddenly Joe felt very sick. He made an effort to call out, but before sound came his elbows slipped from the table's edge with a crash that spilled the remaining cocktails. Richard and Milly stopped dancing and looked at the detective. Richard said, "A great watch-dog our pal turned out to be. Passed out on a half-dozen drinks." He shook his head. "I'd hate like hell to be in a spot and have to depend on him to get me out."

He took Milly by the arm and manipulated the mustache.

"Let's get out of here. This monkey's out for the night. I've got to see the boys at three o'clock."

Milly lifted Joe's head and let it fall with a plump.

"He sure is out. Aren't we going to take him with us?"

Dick grunted. "What do you think, baby?" He was guiding her to the door. "This is where we unload a bad man from the West. West Orange. From now on this Jersey hill-billy is on his own."

Milly giggled. It was the first in several hours. At the door Richard went into a whispered conversation with the bartender. The Syrian nodded and pocketed a bill. He followed the couple to the door and stood there until the roar of the car was lost in the speed of the gale. Then he began closing up for the night.

Chapter Four

THE UNRELENTING, gale-swept rain continued its merciless onslaught. It formed a pool around Joe South and dumped gallons of water on him as he lay unconscious on his back at the bottom of a walk-down service entry.

Joe stirred slightly and shivered. He didn't open his eyes. His head was a ton of vibrating pain and the only part of him that wasn't numb. Eyes still shut, mouth open, he allowed the chilling water to trickle down his throat. After a moment he tried his legs. They were weak at first and he clung helplessly to the bottom step. A police car passed, slowed and drove on. Joe groped for his watch. It was gone. So was his billfold with the two fives it had held. He heaved a sigh as his feeble fingers closed on the six hundred-dollar bills still safely tucked in his shirt pocket. Slowly, with great effort, he climbed the five steps to the street.

He looked around to orient himself. It was no good. He tried to recall just where he had been. The effort, aided by the rain, brought a single lucid memory. Harlem. He couldn't quite focus his blurred gaze but he was certain this street didn't belong to Harlem. For the moment anger almost cleared his head. He'd been carted away from that greasy dive and dumped like any ordinary drunk.

A careful search of his pockets revealed nothing but a soggy package of cigarettes and a nail file. There were no coins. Even his keys were gone. He remembered Carton's topcoat. Its absence brought his first coherent reaction to his position. There was no hat in the entry-way and no stick.

Water swished sluggishly in his shoes as he walked painfully along the sidewalk. Every bone ached and he felt that he could tell exactly where each began and ended. One side of the sign at the corner said 82nd Street and the other said Lexington. Joe heaved a sigh. He walked south on Lexington and west on 78th.

The Raleigh house stood quiet under the downpour. No lights showed. With little hope he pressed the button. Chimes sounded but there was no response. He pushed it again, longer this time and waited another minute. Disgustedly he walked through the drive-way to the rear. The windows along that side were too high to reach from the ground. The rear ones were easier. He was prying at one with the nail file when he noticed that the back door was open. Wide open. Had it been in front it would have been kicked from its hinges by the wind. Here, protected by surrounding buildings, it scarcely moved.

Puzzled, but with a feeling of gratitude for the dry warmth of the interior, Joe entered and closed the door softly behind him. He made immediately for his room. In the bathroom he thrust a finger down his throat and vomited till everything he'd eaten in the last two days was out of his system. A steaming shower followed by icy spray improved him considerably.

With a towel around his stomach he returned to the bedroom. There he climbed into pajamas and bathrobe. In the pockets of the robe he found a Chesterfield package with three cigarettes. Lighting one he switched off the lamp and went to the window where he stood puffing slowly, watching the storm.

What a night! That last drink had been loaded. Once before a bartender in Colon, Canal Zone, had given him a Mickey Finn. The effects were the same, but he had been out longer that time. The museum-piece clock, ticking away on the museum-piece highboy, said five minutes past four. The light on his cigarette inched toward his lips as he moodily deplored his stupidity in underestimating Richard Raleigh. He said under his breath, "I'll have it out with that screwball before I hit the hay."

At that instant the garage in the back of the yard took shape. It was suddenly illuminated by the headlights of a car moving slowly up the driveway. Then several things happened. Somewhere downstairs a door slammed. A second later the figure of a man, caught for an instant in the arc of headlights, darted from the rear of the house to the fence dividing the Raleigh yard from its neighbors. In a flash he was over, falling, it looked, head-first.

The driver of the car had seen it too. Gears ground as the machine reversed and careened recklessly backward into the street. Joe stood at the window as it raced to the end of the block and turned.

Everything had happened in a few split seconds and had come and gone with the rapidity of a momentary flash of lightning. It had been like two or three feet of movie film selected at random from a full-length drama, flickering briefly, then darkness. The cigarette was burning Joe's fingers. He threw the butt into the bowl in the bathroom.

He didn't dally with his hunch. A moment later he was creeping noiselessly along the hall toward the front bedrooms. The hall, lighted by a single wall-bracketed lamp at the head of the stairs, seemed endless. He paused a moment when he thought he heard a faint shuffle like footsteps. He listened, but there was no sound through the closed doors. He turned back. At his left near the rear end of the hall a door stood ajar. Slowly, under the pressure of his elbow it swung inward. He moved in with it to reduce the possibility of being silhouetted against the light in the hallway.

Feeble rays from a street lamp outlined the bed and a recumbent figure. Cautiously he moved nearer. His eyes gradually becoming accustomed to the dim illumination, he saw that the figure was not Richard Raleigh. Long hair, contrasting darkly against the white of the sheets, told him it was a woman.

The woman didn't move as he drew closer. Alcohol, heavy and stale, hung over the bed like marsh gas over a foggy river. When her identity struck him the smile which had been the cue for many Jack Oakie cracks spread involuntarily across his lips. Richard

Raleigh not only knew how to pick them, he knew what to do with them. Milly had probably passed out in a drunken stupor. There usually wasn't much you could do with a woman in that condition. He slipped his left hand carelessly over her shoulder. It was warm under his palm. She didn't stir.

It was then that he suddenly realized something was decidedly wrong. The grin vanished into the semi-darkness of the bedroom as he found her wrist. There was no pulse. He moved his hand slowly below the breasts and withdrew it abruptly. In the thin, rain-filtered light he saw it was sticky with warm blood. Carefully, with the other hand he pulled the covers back. Milly was naked. In the region of her navel was a large, slowly spreading dark spot. Nearly in the center was an ugly blacker patch. *She was very dead.* Joe replaced the covers and turned back to the room.

On the floor beside the bed the evening dress she had worn lay in a heap. Flung across it was a brief step-in and brassiere. Her slippers were under the bed with wet stockings beside them.

Joe paused indecisively. A nauseous odor of death and stale liquor clung about the room and he felt his stomach muscles contract.

He swore softly at the darkness. Sober reasoning warned him to leave things as they were. The luminous dial of an electric clock on a nearby dressing table said four-seventeen. He calculated that he had been in the room no longer than three minutes. With a final look he left, wiping the door knob carefully.

Back in his room he hastily removed the .32 automatic from his suitcase. With it in his right hand, his left still sticky with blood, he made a systematic search of each room on the floor. Then he went through the entire house from basement to garret. Finished, he felt certain that no living soul besides himself remained in the building.

In his own bathroom he washed his hands in the bowl of the commode, drying them with tissue which he flushed down the drain. All traces of blood washed safely away, he removed his pajamas and bathrobe and placed them carefully folded where they had been laid out on the bed. Then gingerly he dressed in wet clothes. When he had finished he examined every inch of the suite to see that everything was as it had been when the maid had left him. Only Carton's coat was missing. He hoped when the police went over the house they would find no evidence that he had returned.

Downstairs in the library he telephoned the hotel. The dull signal rang for what seemed an interminable time before Kierney's sleepy voice answered. Joe was tense.

"Listen, Mick. Just listen. That's all I ask. I want you and Kitch to dress, get Kitch's car and pick me up right away. I'll be walking down the park side of Fifth Avenue somewhere between 78th and

59th. Be there in about twenty minutes. No longer, for heaven's sake! Now don't ask questions and don't answer any on your way up."

Kierney's sleep-filled complaint yawned over the wire.

"What the hell, Joey! What the hell you expect? It's rainin' like hell outside!"

Joe barked into the mouthpiece, "It'll be raining rubber hose at Headquarters if you don't get out. I'll explain when you pick me up. Remember twenty minutes. No longer."

He replaced the receiver against further protests and wiped the instrument free of fingerprints. He found Kierney's reversible in the closet where the maid had put it. He slid into it and let himself into the street.

The storm-battered weather had gained in fury as he turned left on Fifth Avenue. In the park, trees groaned mournfully as their branches swayed and gave ground under the force of the gale. Several cars tearing madly into the teeth of the wind swished past, splashing water from flooded gutters into Joe's face. He swore, then decided to save his breath. He was already wet through and a little more wouldn't make any difference.

He realized it was too soon to expect Kierney and Carton. At 68th Street he stopped and rummaged in his wet pockets for a cigarette.

A taxi, crammed to the floor boards with late revelers, slushed by. One of its occupants heaved an empty whisky bottle drunkenly from the window. Joe ducked. It crashed against a wall two feet from his head. Following immediately behind the cab was a large black sedan. It pulled up fifty feet ahead of him and came to a stop at the curb. Joe ran for it. The rear door opened. Joe said, "I thought you guys would never . . ."

He didn't finish. His hand shot under the reversible too late. He was looking into the round, bright eye of a small pearl-handled revolver. The driver of the car was Frankie Shasta. He said, "Come een outa da rain, Meester Sout'."

Joe did. In the rear seat was Porky Wiener. One of his fat hands, the one with the gun in it, was in Joe's ribs. The other slid under the reversible and came out with Joe's .32. The car started off. Without turning Shasta said, "On da floor, pleeze, Meester Sout'."

Porky said nothing. Joe got off the seat and crawled painfully to the floor. The fat man obligingly lifted his feet for him, to lie down and replaced them down on Joe's ankles. The man weighed a ton. The revolver was now leveled at his head, which was quite unnecessary. With Porky's weight on his legs he couldn't have moved himself with a crowbar.

The sedan continued down Fifth Avenue, its windshield wiper tick-tacking a monotonous rhythm in defiance of the rain. Once Shasta turned from the driver's seat to say, "Put your nose on da floor, pleeze, Meester Sout'."

Joe groaned and rolled over. The car was headed south on Fifth Avenue, he was sure. Porky's revolver was still aimed at his head. As the car stopped for a red light he said into the rug, "This is a snatch, Shasta. You know what that means?"

Shasta didn't answer. Porky did. He brought one foot over and deposited it with a thud on the back of the detective's head. Joe groaned, "You son of a . . ."

The foot came down again. Blood from his nose trickled into the rug. He kept quiet after that. The sedan continued down Fifth Avenue for a few more blocks and turned right. Five minutes later it made a very short left turn. It came to a stop with the motor running.

There was the sound of a steel garage door being raised. The machine moved forward again and halted about twenty yards inside the building. The motor was cut off this time and Joe heard the protesting creak of the door as it was lowered.

Shasta got out. Then for an agonizing moment Joe thought his legs were going through the floor boards as Porky rested his full weight on them before he stepped out.

Shasta's voice, oiled with high-test lubricant, was gentle. "Weel you pleeze step out from da car, Meester Sout'?"

Joe massaged his aching legs. Blood from his nose salted his lips. Shasta, with the tenderness of a father, helped him out and led him to a chair. A third man, a dark, wiry Sicilian, was leaning against the wall picking his teeth. Joe had only a moment to observe his surroundings before Shasta spoke to the Sicilian.

"Tony, geeve Meester Sout' a leetle someteeng to pap him op," he ordered.

Tony disappeared into a room partitioned with beaver board and wire chicken fencing. He returned almost immediately with a partially filled bottle of Scotch which he handed silently to Joe. Joe took a long drink. The warm liquor reacted according to Shasta's prescription. He felt considerably better. The Italian watched him as he drank. Porky, gun in hand, hadn't once relaxed his vigil. The room, which Joe judged to be on the ground floor of a warehouse, was lighted by a single 100-watt lamp. Piled almost to the ceiling were cases of liquor bearing brand labels of many well-known distilleries. He took another drink. Shasta waited patiently. Joe said, "You Scotch people certainly make excellent whisky."

Shasta studied him closely. He didn't smile.

"Meester Sout', dese Scotch she import' from da ol' contry."

Joe tried a grin.

"Is that what you call Brooklyn since you came to Manhattan? I suppose this stuff ages seven years crossing Williamsburg Bridge."

Shasta ignored that.

"Meester Sout', on da way over here you say someteeng aboud keednapeeng. Is dat right?"

Joe nodded. "And it's a plenty good break for you that you didn't decide to move me to Jersey. Ever hear of the Lindbergh Law? As it is you'll probably only get life."

Shasta's eyes narrowed as though pondering the possibilities of a life sentence. There was the faintest trace of a grin under the professionally trimmed mustache.

"And who, my fran', ees going to tell da poleeze about keednapeeng? You don't look so domb."

Joe's grin was bleak.

"Thanks for the compliment. I'm going easy on you, Shasta. I appreciate those slugs of bum Scotch, but if I have anything to say about it the police are going to build a pen around that fat . . . Gargantua there is going to spend the rest of his life eating off the end of a pitchfork." Joe rubbed his still aching legs.

Shasta wasn't amused. "You plenty domb," he grunted.

"Woll, you ought to know nobody gets away with a snatch," Joe reminded him.

"Not even when da keednaped fellow he's a murderah?" Shasta's eyebrows reached his hairline. "Dat was a dirty treek, Meester Sout' —keeling leetle Meely dat way."

Joe leaped out of the chair, "She was already dead . . ." he stopped abruptly and sank back. Too late he realized he had walked flatfootedly into the trap. Shasta sighed, flicking a strand of hair from the satin lapel of his evening jacket.

"But you know Meely, she dad?"

The blood rose in Joe's face. His anger at his own blunder mounted with his antagonism toward the ice-tempered Shasta. His tone climbed a couple of notes as he flung a finger at the other.

"Listen, you oily-tongued sonofa . . . Sure, *I* know she's dead. I saw her. But nobody's pinning that on me."

Shasta remained unperturbed.

"Sure, sure," he agreed. "You didn't keel her. We believe you. You come out from da house. Meely she dad. Nobody else in da house. No-h-h. You didn't keel leetle Meely."

Joe wiped coagulated blood from his nose. Porky and the man called Tony brought their chairs closer. He repeated between dry lips, "I didn't kill her."

Shasta took a mechanical pencil from the pocket of a richly brocaded vest and became absorbed in extending and retracting the lead. He didn't look up.

"Meester Sout', we *are* sorry for leetle Meely, she dad. We are sorry for you, you keeled her, but dat is not why we breeng you here. We want you should tell what you do wit' Deeky Raleigh."

Joe's surprise reached a new high. This time he had no intention of skidding on the foreigner's oil.

"I haven't seen that double-crossing screwball since he laid me out with a Mickey last night. When I do lay my hands on him I'll do plenty 'wit' heem.' "

Shasta skipped the mimic.

"Meester Sout', Deeky Raleigh he's got ten t'ousan' dollar he should have deleever for my company tonight. Deeky he is honest boy. Maybe he double-cross you, but he don't do it to me. When he collect for me he pay me. He don' run away. What did you do wit' Deeky, Meester Sout'?"

Joe shouted, "I don't know where he is! I don't know where your money is! I don't know where a darned thing is! He's probably bumped Milly and took a powder with the dough," he added desperately.

He knew the last statement was ridiculous. Richard Raleigh, with a fortune coming to him in two months, would hardly be foolish enough to run off with ten thousand dollars. Shasta said it aloud. "No, Deeky don' run away wit' da money. Deeky not crazy lak dat." He added for good measure, "Maybe you keel Deeky too, huh?"

"Oh, heavens!" was all Joe could manage.

Frankie Shasta straightened from where he had been leaning casually against a pilaster. Without taking his eyes from the pencil, he said with deadly menace, "You don' going to tell us what you do wit' Deeky? I t'ink you do. You badder talk now."

"Look here," Joe said desperately. "Let's start from the beginning. Let me tell you exactly what happened today."

He began with his visit to Van Pelt, his meeting with the older Raleigh and his subsequent arrival at the Raleigh house. He went on to his late meeting with Richard and described in detail the party which followed. He complained bitterly about the Mickey Finn, and finally he told how he had found Milly's body. He didn't mention having telephoned Kierney and Carton. He knew Shasta and Wiener would know most of the story by morning anyway, but what they wouldn't know wouldn't hurt them. It might conceivably do Joe a lot of harm. When he had finished he turned to Shasta.

"So you see, Richard was nowhere around. Completely gone."

Shasta, still without looking up, and with infinite patience said, "What did you do wit' da money?"

"Meester Sout', what is going to happen to you I can't look at. I can't stand blood and holler. I hope you tell Meester Wiener what you do wit' da money. Meester Wiener is maybe badder dan me." Shasta looked genuinely sad as he crossed the room and got into the sedan. He closed both doors.

The detective turned to Porky Wiener. The fat man had not uttered a word either during the ride or the interview. He sat like a poker-faced Buddha, the pearl-handled revolver still in his blubbery hand. Porky motioned Tony, who approached with a length of rope. Recalling Kierney's colorful description of Wiener, Joe made no effort to resist. The rope in the hands of an expert soon became a strait-jacket while he lay helpless on the floor. Tony produced the Scotch and drank deeply. Joe decided he was fortifying himself against whatever was to follow. He wondered how Porky's efforts to learn what he didn't know would differ from the gentle Shasta.

He didn't have to wait. The ponderous Wiener lifted his three hundred and fifty pounds slowly from the chair and lumbered over. He stood looking down without expression. Then without warning he acted. The pachyderm leg rose slowly and the heel came down with sickening force on the detective's stomach. For the second time that morning he lost consciousness.

When he came to Tony was pouring water on his face. Then came the Scotch. Joe swallowed carefully with Tony holding his head. The liquor burned his throat. Porky was seated again. No emotion stirred his fat face. Nausea gripped Joe. The walls became the ceiling, then the floor. Porky left his chair again and stood over him. Joe swore hysterically. He saw the leg rising slowly. Screaming, he tried to roll over. There was no light. Porky came down. All of him. Only a part of him fell on Joe. There was the sound of a car door opening and a dull thud which might have been a falling body.

Joe was still half-sobbing, half-swearing when he realized the ropes were being loosened. There was still no light. He was frightened. Maybe there was a light and he couldn't see it. The man over him was working quietly. He bent over Joe's ear. "I warned you them . . . was tough." It was Kierney.

Joe lay free of the ropes, gasping fitfully. He said, "Crack open one of those cases against the wall."

Kierney complied. Joe was in no mood to dispute the quality this time. It, together with Kierney, helped him unsteadily to his feet. He whispered hoarsely, "Let's get out of here."

Kierney, bracing him, led him through a side door and into the rear seat of Carton's sedan. He rubbed his stomach weakly. "Where's Kitch?" he finally managed to ask.

"Looking things over," Kierney grunted. "We'd of knocked them monkeys out sooner only Kitch had a helluva lot of trouble with that door. It don't open easy like it looked. You sit here a minute, uunstan'? That place gives me an idea."

He disappeared into the garage. A minute later Kitch appeared. He had a flashlight and carried Porky's pistol in his right hand. He tossed Joe a brief glance and climbed in behind the wheel.

"Sorry we didn't get in sooner. Where's Kierney?"

Before Joe could answer the Irishman moved toward them carefully holding on to a large bundle wrapped in newspapers. He said, "What the hell. Them monkeys'll never miss two bottles. And if they do, what? That ain't all I got," he added as he settled himself next to Carton.

Out of respect for his aching stomach and throbbing head Joe tried hard to suppress a laugh. It didn't work. It was the first belly laugh he'd had in twenty-four hours and it hurt like hell.

Chapter Five

THE BIG SEDAN sped north on Second Avenue. Carton was driving and next to him Kierney balanced the bundle carefully on his lap. Joe in the rear seat watched the el pillars swish past. He was not too far gone to note the location of the warehouse from which he had been rescued. No one had spoken during the hurried departure. At 38th Street, Carton slowed and spoke over his shoulder.

"Where now, Public Enemy?" His voice was tinged with mockery.

Painfully Joe straightened to a more comfortable position.

"I guess May's apartment is the safest place. She lives in Gloucester Tower on East 43rd Street, but better drive around to the First Avenue entrance. It'll do until I can think of something. How'd you find me?"

"It was quite simple," Carton chuckled. "And if you'd waited another minute you'd have spared yourself all that punishment. You're too impatient by far, Joey. We saw you get in Shasta's car. We figured something was wrong, but we had to follow at a safe distance. And, incidentally, the lock on that door gave me considerable trouble. I meant to look into it more closely." He slowed for a traffic signal. "May we be permitted to know, Joey, what the blazes you did to get those gentlemen so angry with you?"

Joe shrugged and swore disgustedly.

"They thought I'd bumped Dick's girl."

"The hell you say." Kierney almost upset the bottle. "Did you, Joey?"

"No, but I might as well have. She's dead, all right. I found her in young Raleigh's bed with a hole in her belly big enough to drive this jallopy through."

For the second time in as many hours Joe went over the incidents leading up to the murder. He began with the time he left Carton and Kierney the evening before and related in detail his meeting with Dick and Naomi through to the moment he was picked up by the two racketeers at a little after four-thirty that morning.

"What's worrying me right now is where the hell *is* our problem child? It's more than possible that he killed Milly, but it doesn't jell. In the first place, why? Secondly, why in *his* bedroom? In the third place, why again? It doesn't click. On the other hand, if he didn't kill her what's the set-up that makes his absence necessary? He may have had guts enough to kill Milly but not enough to double-cross Shasta and his man-mountain persuader. I'm convinced Dick went back to the house with Milly. She wouldn't have gone there alone. I'm also sure it wasn't Dick who went over the fence and out. The whole thing is cock-eyed and it's going to take more than John Kieran or a Philadelphia lawyer to walk in with the answers."

"Quite," Carton agreed. "And from what you tell me, Mildred Evans doesn't fit in at all. If she was shot to keep her mouth shut, by whom and why? Certainly those toughs wouldn't put their heads in a noose just for ten thousand dollars. Besides, that kind of business went out with Prohibition."

"Well," Joe sounded resigned, "we *were* under the impression that Repeal would eliminate the bootlegging racket, too. However"—he shrugged disgustedly—"I'm still on the job to watch that double-crossing little squirt and I'm going to find him, cops or no cops. I'm in a pretty swell spot. If I'm tossed in the clink I won't be any use to anybody." He caressed his aching stomach. "One thing I'm pretty sure of is that Milly was wise to Dick's relations with Wiener and Shasta. Before she knew my identity she almost gave me the set-up. She wasn't quite drunk enough though."

"I thought that retainer Van Pelt shelled out was a trifle generous for the kind of job it was," Carton remarked at large as they turned right on 42nd Street to First Avenue.

Trucks lumbered desolately over the rough brick paving, and as Carton drew up in front of the rear entrance to Gloucester Tower the shrill sound of an ambulance cut the thick atmosphere as it raced toward Bellevue. Avoiding the elevators the three men climbed four floors to May's apartment, Kierney still carrying the loot from the warehouse. Joe rang the bell. There was no answer. He rang again and picked up a pint of cream outside the door. A second later May's voice answered sleepily.

"It's your own personal milkman, Babe," Joe announced. Her voice flowed through the transom less sleepily this time.

"Go home, Joey. You're drunk. Do you realize it's not eight o'clock yet? And how many times have I told you not to call me Babe?" She sounded annoyed.

"Aw, honey," Joe pleaded. "It's important. I must see you."

"That's what you always say when you're drunk, Joey. Go home and let me finish my beauty sleep. This is a fine time to lumber in on a decent girl."

An elevator stopped on their floor and voices came down the corridor. Carton pushed Joe aside and produced a bunch of keys. They were inside before the early comers swung into sight. Joe slid past Carton toward the bedroom. May was standing in the doorway clutching a pale azure dressing gown about her. As Joe approached she opened her lips to scream. He put his hand over her mouth.

"For the luvva Mike, honey, this is serious!"

From the shapely leg revealed through the open front of the dressing gown it was easy to guess the rest of May. She was as streamlined as a Petty drawing. She didn't look as dumb. Her body silhouetted through the close-fitting garment was as smooth as a model's. It was a model's. May worked for one of the largest model agencies in New York.

Joe came to the point. "I'm in a jam, May," he said simply.

She was belatedly tying the cord of her dressing gown.

"You're always in a jam," she reminded him. "You've got some on your face now. How did you get in?"

"Carton's magic keys." He looked at his face in the mirror of the door. One side of it was covered with dried blood from his nose. May picked up the telephone on the night table. She said, "Well, here's where you get unloaded. And, who, by the way, is Carton?"

"Aw, May," Joe ignored the question and slapped his hand over the mouthpiece. "Don't do that, honey. I tell you I'm in a spot. A hell of a spot. I may get a murder rap hung on me."

May was sleepy. She was also very mad.

"And a leopard never changes its spots!" she snapped. Then her expression changed from annoyance to terror and she sat down suddenly on the bed. Joe slid down beside her and put his arms around her.

"Now listen for a minute, honey. I'm on a job and it's all messed up with murder." Quickly he outlined the main facts. He took advantage of her momentary sympathy to dramatize the beating he had taken from Wiener and Shasta. When he had finished May looked at him suspiciously without speaking. Reassured by his pallor and the tired lines around his eyes she took him by the hand to the bathroom. With the first touch of cold water on his face Joe relaxed and sighed, "May, you're an angel."

May's husky voice said close to his ear, "An angel when you're in a jam. And your life is one great mountain of it. You wallow in it from year to year. Do you realize you haven't called me for over a week?"

Joe said again, "You're an angel."

She was patting white cream on his face and smoothing it into his skin with the tenderness of a mother. She pressed closer and whispered, "Does your stomach still hurt?"

"You said it, honey." Joe put his arm around her. "It hurts like hell."

May laughed softly.

"Well, you'll have to take care of that yourself." She poked him in the ribs with her finger and left the bathroom.

He stripped and stepped gingerly under the shower.

As he opened the bathroom door a welcome aroma of coffee and frying bacon hit his nose.

He found his underwear, which had escaped most of the rain's onslaught, and May had laid out an old beach robe he had left there the summer before. He felt almost comfortable.

She was setting the table in the living room and he saw that she was already dressed for the street.

"May," he began in a confidential voice, "I'm damned sorry to have to drag you into this, but it's the only way. We've got to use your place for the next couple of days. At least until this business is cleaned up. Every cop in town will be on my tail. We're hiding out, May. I haven't asked you for many favors. Won't you please be a little considerate?"

"Considerate! *You* talk about consideration! Suppose they do catch up with you and in my apartment? Consideration! Won't I look lovely posing with you and your baby pandas? And with steel bars between me and the flash bulbs!" She took a final sip of coffee and rose. "All I can say is this, I want you three out of here when I get back this afternoon."

Joe jumped up and held her wrists.

"May, get this. We're stopping here. I'll pay your hotel bill anywhere you say, but we stay here."

She freed one hand and brought it up to the side of his face. The smack could have been heard at Grand Central.

"Who do you think you are?" she flared. "You Hell's Kitchen Hitler! Telling me what to do in my own apartment!"

Joe sat down on the davenport. His cheek hurt. His nose had started bleeding again.

May jerked out a handkerchief and applied it gently to his nose. Her anger vanished as quickly as it had come.

She said, "I'm terribly sorry, Joey, but you do make me so darned mad. You expect the most impossible things. First, you wanted me to harbor a negro schizophrenic; then it was that Martin baby, and one time you even brought a cage of snakes up here. The next thing I know you'll be using this for a Bund headquarters." She paused and a tear trickled down her cheek. She said in a milder tone. "Of course, you *can* stay here, but please try to keep out of sight. I guess there's enough room for all of us. I'll call you later."

Joe looked over his handkerchief. His voice was nasal.

"May, you're an angel."

She went toward the bedroom. A few minutes later she returned carrying a raincoat, umbrella and a large hatbox of the sort used by models to carry their changes. With her hand on the doorknob she said to Joe, "When your pals settle down just ask them to keep their dirty feet off my new sofa."

Kierney let out the breath he'd been holding for the last five minutes. "Whew-w-w," he whistled. "What a woman!"

"What a man!" Joe chuckled, but his face was still red. He became serious immediately and shrugged resignedly. "Now what do we do? This mess has me going around in circles."

"We might," Carton reminded him, "examine the loot for a start. Clear the table, Mick, and drag it over."

"Yeah," Joe said. "When that dame's been found, her torso before and aft will be on every front page by the *Times*."

Carton set his cup down.

"But even the *Times* will carry a nice big beautiful picture of Joe South," he drawled. "And he's going to be the most popular public enemy on Manhattan Island."

Joe said, "Never had a good one made."

Kierney reached for the newspaper in which the bottles had been wrapped. As he picked it up a number of miscellaneous articles spilled over the table. There were two billfolds, Shasta's mechanical pencil and two bunches of keys. Joe picked up the first of the billfolds. Under the celluloid window was a snapshot of Shasta and a not too beautiful synthetic blonde. It also contained seven hundred-dollar bills, two twenties and some singles. Joe laid it carefully aside and reached for the other one.

It was Wiener's. It held a checkbook and fourteen dollars in bills. In the change pocket was fifteen cents and a small circular tin box. Joe looked at solemnly and tossed it to Kierney.

"Something for your hope chest, Casanova."

Carton was carefully examining the bills from the fat man's pockets. He looked up as Joe sat down.

"What about the wireless, Joey?" he suggested. Joe moved to the radio and dialed nervously. A carefully cultured voice was describing a formula for dessert. Joe turned the knob disgustedly. A Brooklyn politician was just finishing a speech. They listened and a minute later a newscaster took the air. Twelve minutes of European war news, interspersed with sports and a local fire went by before they heard what they were waiting for.

"Police of the entire Metropolitan area are searching for the murderer of an unidentified young woman whose nude, bullet-riddled body was found at an early hour this morning in the home of the wealthy Wall Street broker, Parker Hayden Raleigh, on East 78th Street. The body was discovered in the bedroom of Richard Raleigh, nephew of Parker Raleigh, by Precious Lamb, a negro maid, who telephoned the police after seeking advice from friends in Harlem.

"Sought for questioning by police are young Richard Raleigh and Joe South, one-time private investigator, who, according to the boy's uncle, was acting as companion and bodyguard to his nephew.

"The elder Raleigh, recuperating from a nervous disorder at a local hospital, was in a state of collapse after being advised of the crime. He has been unable to make a further statement.

"You have been listening . . ."

Joe switched the radio off. No one spoke. The detective shrugged.

"Well, that's that. I can't figure it. I'm sure Shasta and Wiener are stooges for somebody who's dumping bootleg liquor around town. They're probably using Dick for a front and come-on. Likewise, he's collected the dough." He frowned. "That part's easy. I had that figured last night. Where the hell *is* Dick, and, quoting Shasta's theme song, where's da ten t'ousan' dollar? It's ridiculous to think he killed Milly. He's not the type to kill for the sake of unrequited passion. Besides, if he were, it wouldn't be Milly. Nothing unrequited about that set-up."

He scratched his head. Neither Kierney nor Carton spoke. Carton reached down and picked up the Siamese which had entered and was brushing against his leg. It spoke in a small trusting voice and snuggled in the crook of his arm. Joe stared.

"Kitch, I have to hand it to you. You certainly have a way with the ladies. That's the first time I've ever known smudge-face to make friends with a stranger."

Carton's smile was lazy. "Remind me sometime to instruct you in the psychology of cats," he drawled. "Right now I'm too tired to think." He nodded toward Kierney. The Irishman had relaxed in the only comfortable chair in the room and was exploding sounds like a saw through knotty hickory. "He has the right idea."

"More power to him," Joe said. "But this thing has me nuts. How did Shasta and Wiener know I'd be coming out of the 78th Street house at that special time? How did they know Milly was dead? I know damn well there wasn't a soul in that place after I got through with it. In the same peculiar way they knew Dick wasn't there. Even if it was their car in the driveway, and I think it was, they still had no way of knowing what had happened inside." He paused and ran a hand through his hair. "I'm sure everybody that has anything to do with the Timbuctoo is tied up with the business some way. Otherwise, how did they get wise to me so quickly? It's true I knew that blonde hatcheck when she was a cigarette girl at the Zero Club."

He looked at the Englishman and grinned when he saw that he, too, was sound asleep. He shrugged, said, "What the hell?" and slid further down on the end of the davenport.

Chapter Six

JOE GROANED and struggled up from the tunnel of a nightmare. The welcome sound which had rescued him was a key turning in a lock. He lifted himself up. It took only a second for his mind to register. He rose shakily, his heart pounding, as May entered. He glanced instinctively at his wrist and remembered that his watch was gone.

"Babe! It's you. You sure startled me. Why didn't you telephone first?" He blinked stupidly.

"And why should I? Haven't you learned that bells make Goggles nervous?" She shrugged out of the slicker and tossed her hat across the room. She looked at Joe suspiciously. "It's only a trifle, of course, but have you solved the Great Gun Mystery? It's twelve o'clock and you've had plenty of time."

Joe turned to see Carton getting to his feet. It still surprised him the way the Englishman slept and awoke without seeming to do either. Kierney was snoring. Goggles had jumped from Carton's lap at the sound of May's voice and was now perched on her shoulder purring contentedly.

"And what have you there, lassie?" Carton pointed to the folded newspaper May still held in her hand.

"Just wait, me lads." May's voice was calm, but there was suppressed excitement in her eyes as she sat down beside Joe.

"Out with it, Babe," he prompted her.

"All right, all right. Don't press me. And I'd suggest you wake Carnera there so we'll save breath."

Joe pushed Kierney off the chair. The Irishman floundered and came up shadow-boxing. "What the hell?" he shouted.

"Quiet, mug. May's got news."

Kierney rubbed his eyes and clambered back into the chair.

May settled herself on the couch and took a deep breath. "In a word, Brain Trust, they've found Dick Raleigh."

Joe grabbed her arm. "Where?"

In the garage back of his house." She thrust the folded paper at him. "Read it and weep."

It was the *Daily Record*, and across the top in banner lines Joe read:

BODY OF RICHARD RALEIGH FOUND IN GARAGE

The search for Richard Raleigh, which began with the finding of the body of Mildred Evans in his bedroom ths morning, came to a close when his bullet-riddled body was discovered at nine-fifteen by Detective Sergeant Francis A. Doheny. Sergeant Doheny stated that he had gone to the garage to check on Raleigh's car. The position of the dead boy, slumped over the wheel, indicated that he had backed the machine into the garage and was on the point of getting out when he was attacked.

Sergeant Doheny further stated that Raleigh had apparently been taken by surprise. Absence of fingerprints on the car led police to the conclusion that the murderer had lain in wait for his victim. No weapon was found. Bullets removed from the body were from a .32 automatic pistol.

The dead boy's body was taken to the City morgue where it was formally identified by Miss Naomi Raleigh, sister of the deceased. Miss Raleigh was in no condition to be questioned at length. She told police she knew of no one who might have wanted to kill her brother.

That the killing is tied up with the murder of Mildred Evans police are positive. Fingerprints, identified as those of the dead girl, found on an extension telephone in the upper hallway of the Raleigh house, led police to believe that she was attacked while trying to telephone for help.

Search is still under way for Joe South, one-time private investigator, who is alleged to have been acting as bodyguard for Richard Raleigh. . . .

Joe came to the end of the page and grunted. "So there it is," he stated disgustedly. "Little Joey's got more jam on his face."

"Oh, yes," May agreed. "It can't be said that you do things halfway, darling, once you get started."

Carton slid onto the davenport. May pushed him with her elbow. "Don't do that, my fine Raffles. You'll disturb Goggles."

"Ladies first," he said as Goggles transferred her perch to his shoulder. May stared.

"Well, you *did* make a hit. She's particular, she is."

"Good heavens!" Joe grumbled. "Are you two will-o-the-wisps gonna talk about smudge-face while I sit here waiting for the hangman?"

May lit a cigarette. "Keep your temper down, Joey," she warned. "Besides, it's the electric chair in this state. I have more information you may be interested in. Your friend, Mr. Van Pelt, and his secretary were among those present at the Timbuctoo last night."

Joe slumped. "Where'd you get that?" he demanded.

"From one of the girls at the studio. You remember the red-head you always ogle so disgustingly. She sat at the table next to them."

"Oh!" Light dawned on Joe. "So that's who she was. How'd she know it was Martha Lane?"

"Elementary, my good Watson. Elementary." May gave him a suspicious scowl. "And, by the way, big shot, she said you were doing a pretty good burlesque with the Evans girl. What about it? While I sit here reading Gertrude Stein you're out struggling with the intelligentsia. Martha Lane had her Beacon Hill accent turned on full force. Only as the drinks increased the accent diminished."

Joe chuckled. "Slipped on her broad A's, huh? What the hell do you suppose *they* were doing there?"

"*I* wouldn't know," Carton said. "Probably sampling the real bonded stuff."

"I mean why would Van Pelt choose last night to be there? He's not the kind of guy to hang around dumps like that."

"I don't suppose for a minute he is—normally." Carton clipped the last word as though glad to be rid of it.

"What do you mean?"

"Only that there must have been something unusual afoot for him to be there at all. Why don't you ask him? That is, if you two are still on speaking terms. The untimely demise of young Dick sort of puts you on the spot two ways, you know."

Joe looked down at the beach robe.

"This would be a nice outfit to be pinched in," he said dryly. "What did you do with my pants, May?"

"Nice question to ask a respectable girl," she sniffed and flicked ashes in a tray. "You couldn't wear them as they were, Joey, so I sent them down to be cleaned. That much for my reputation." She snapped her fingers. "The bellboy probably thinks I'm modeling an oversized Dietrich by this time."

Kierney, who had been quiet, yawned and observed in a bored voice, "Why can't we have a drink and some grub?"

Joe grunted. "That's where all your brains are, dope. In your stomach." He rubbed his own. "But for once you've had an idea."

"If there's anything left," May agreed. "I doubt it with you three wolves on the wrong side of the door."

Kierney was filling the tea kettle when the boy returned with Joe's clothes. May tossed him a package as he started for the bedroom.

"Don't say I don't think of you once in a while, Joey. You'll find a shirt and socks in there, and it isn't my fault if they don't come up to your sartorial requirements. It's the best I could do on short notice."

Joe breathed a sigh for the wits God had given May and disappeared into the bedroom. He dressed in record time and returned to find the table set and smell the appetizing odor of broiling steak.

"I like your taste in shirts, Angel," he told May.

May placed a platter of bread on the table and gave him an appraising glance. "I've been waiting for an excuse to change those race-track colors for a long time, sonny," she observed and reached up to flick his tie into place.

"You wouldn't consider that as a lifetime job, would you, honey?" he whispered hopefully as his lips brushed the firm surface. Color flamed for a moment under her fine skin and she lowered her eyes.

Carton's voice came from the kitchen.

"When you two love-birds are through we'll eat." He came through the door as May withdrew her hand.

"Love-birds," she scoffed. "This big baboon is just getting ready to ask another favor. I know the signs." The moment had passed and Joe sighed.

They seated themselves around the crowded card table. When their plates had been filled Carton said, "You know, Joe, right now this whole thing looks like a large, inextricable jigsaw with lots of missing pieces. The Timbuctoo is the key to the color scheme, but somehow it doesn't fit. Mildred Evans' death doesn't tie in with anything. Dick Raleigh's murder is more logical. There could be a dozen reasons for someone wanting him out of the way. Several people," he added and studied his fork thoughtfully.

"Yeah," Joe agreed. "And it looks like the cops think the same person did both jobs. And no matter how much we smart-crack about Mr. Valentine's storm troopers, there isn't much they miss."

"And if you ask me," Kierney put in, "that guy Van Pelt don't look kosher to me. A guy with his dough don't go to joints like the

Timbuctoo with his floozy secretary."

"He does if he pays her apartment rent."

Joe brightened. "How do you know that, Babe?"

"Oh, I get around, and one of the models"—she looked at Joe balefully—"the red-headed one—lives in the same building with Martha Lane. At the most, Miss Lane makes thirty dollars a week, and those apartments set you back a hundred a month. It shouldn't take a master mind to get the right answer."

Joe grinned. "And how does red-head manage to pay for a hundred-dollar apartment?"

"Pipe down, dope. You *would* want to know that. We aren't concerned with her right now. But," she leaned closer and whispered sepulchrally, "if you must know, she's on Hitler's pay roll. She's really a spy."

Kierney's eyes were round and bright. "Naw-w-w!"

Joe said, "Joke," and looked at May. "So that's what she was doing with Coats and Suits the other night." He grinned at Kierney. "Joke again."

Carton said, "Are we trying to solve a murder or write a three-act flop for Broadway next season?"

Joe was serious as he stood up. "All this is very nice and cozy, but it's not getting me anywhere." He turned suddenly and thrust a finger under Kierney's nose. "Did you kill Mildred Evans, tough guy?"

Kierney leered. "How d'ya get that way, Joey? I don't *kill* 'em."

"Skip it. I was just rehearsing for my act with Van Pelt." He looked at the clock. "It's only one-thirty. We might catch the guy at his office. I'm going to have a little talk with that high-powered Dutchman, and it's not going to have anything to do with my will. Coming, Carton?"

"Hey, what about me?" Kierney rose.

"What, indeed?" Carton gave Kierney a push. "You stay here and mount guard on Goggles and Miss Sands. Did it ever occur to you that Shasta and Wiener aren't through with Joe yet? If they discovered our hiding place they'd like nothing better than a chance to use Miss Sands to pry open Joe's mouth. They don't take interference lying down."

Joe brushed the top of May's head with his lips as he went toward the door. "Keep your chin up, Babe," he cautioned as he and Carton let themselves into the hall.

Carton's car was still parked at the curb, apparently undisturbed. It was one-forty-five when they skidded to a stop in front of the building which housed Van Pelt's office. Rain still pattered the sidewalks and damp pedestrians bumped each other with umbrellas as they exited from the skyscraper. Carton stood outside the door of the drug store while Joe went in. The detective found an unoccupied telephone booth and put a coin in the slot. Carefully covering the mouthpiece with his handkerchief he waited. A moment later the Beacon Hill accent uncoiled over the wire. Joe asked for Van Pelt in a high, peevish voice.

"No. Mr. Van Pelt is not here." Martha Lane sounded uncertain. "He's gone for the afternoon. Who's calling, please?"

Joe squeaked again, "It's urgent. I must speak to him immediately. Where can I reach him?"

"I'm sorry, he won't be back this afternoon. Will you leave a message?"

Joe said, "I'll call his home," and hung up. Carton still lounged against the door. Joe walked up. The outer office was empty except for the bored secretary. He said breathlessly, "Hello, Beacon Hill."

"Joey," she squealed. Vermilion-tipped fingers went to her lips. The next moment they reached for the telephone. Joe beat her to it.

"No sense calling the police, toots. I'm here on business. After all, I'm still on his pay roll. Where is he?"

"He'll be here in a minute *with* the police. You haven't a chance, Joey."

Joe gave her credit for the bluff. He said, "I have a chance, but I'm *not* interested. Is that the way you begin with Van Pelt? It must be a good show."

"What do you mean?" She glared venomously. "Some day, Joe South, you are going just a little too far."

"Oh-h-h no, sister. Not me. I go for blondes. Natural blondes. You know, the kind with brains. There isn't anything below that top button there"—he touched the neck of her blouse—"that I'd take the trouble to unfasten it for. And," he added, "not much above it."

"I could kill you—you—you—" she sputtered.

"Now, now, shug, calm down. There's been enough bloodshed already. *That's* what I came up here to talk to Van Pelt about. I thought he might take my case if they hang a murder rap on me."

The pseudo-culture crept back into her voice.

"You'll need all the lawyers in New York to get you out of this mess, Joe. This is murder."

"Sure it is, toots, but Van Pelt hired me to take care of that guy. Not murder him. Somebody else did that. When do you expect him?"

"He ought to be back any minute now," she told him. "Make yourself at home. The state'll be paying for the space you'll occupy soon."

"Then I'll have a drink." He turned as he moved toward Van Pelt's private office. "Oh, by the way, did you and the boss have a good time at the Timbuctoo last night?"

"How did you . . . ?" She caught herself. "We weren't there last night."

"Don't tell me the papers can be wrong," he retorted. As he opened the door into the other office the telephone rang. He picked up the instrument on Van Pelt's desk. The secretary's back was to him. The two receivers lifted together. There were two accents this time. The first one said, "Stuyvesant Van Pelt's office." The other belonged to Frankie Shasta. It said, "Ees Meester Van Pelt there?"

Martha Lane called him Frankie and fixed an appointment for ten o'clock the following morning. The receivers came down together.

Joe found the bottle of Scotch in a filing cabinet. It looked familiar and he brought it closer to the light. As far as he could see it was an exact duplicate of the two bottles Kierney had filched from the warehouse. An excellent imitation of an excellent brand of Scotch. So Van Pelt got his liquor from Shasta and Wiener.

The silver tray and glasses were still on the desk. He poured a stiff shot and swallowed it slowly. It tasted like the McCoy. He was smacking his lips when Martha Lane appeared in the doorway. She looked at Joe hesitantly. Some of the former bravado was missing.

"What did you say about newspapers?"

"I said don't tell me they are wrong."

"Which paper?" she persisted.

"All of them," Joe said. The telephone rang. Joe slipped the Scotch under his coat. The secretary reached the instrument first. She listened and handed it to him. "For you, Joey."

It was Carton. His voice was hurried. "Van Pelt's on his way up. Still want to see him?"

"That requires a lot of talking. You'd better speak to Miss Lane." He handed her the receiver and disappeared down the stairway. Carton kept the secretary in meaningless conversation until Joe arrived. He hung up with a "Cheer-o" in the middle of a sentence. Joe said, "Thanks for catching on. I trapped her into admitting she and her boss were at the Timbuctoo last night. I thought I'd wait to talk with Van Pelt. They'll get together now and fix a *good* story. The double-crossing screwball."

Carton was thoughtful as he slammed the car door.

"You know, Joey, it's just possible that Van Pelt himself had a hand in this business. He's one of the trustees, isn't he? And it looks like he's riding high right now. Otherwise he wouldn't risk being seen openly at a place like the Timbuctoo with Martha Lane."

Joe produced the bottle of Scotch and handed it to Carton.

"See what you think of that, Kitch. It *tastes* like that stuff Tony gave me at the warehouse last night."

Carton swallowed slowly.

49

"Not bad, Joe. Like your Prohibition stuff. What's the idea?"

"I just filched that bottle from Van Pelt's private stock. And while I was up there who should telephone but our dainty little sidekick, Frankie Shasta. It begins to jell."

"What do you mean?"

"This is the way I've figured it. Shasta and Wiener are bootlegging this liquor. Doing a fair job, too, if I'm any judge. They're furnishing the strong-arm stuff and taking chances Van Pelt's supplying the brains and protection and taking the big dough. Richard was stooge number three. It's been a good setup. No fuss or rough stuff to arouse the local cops. Ergo: no Federal interference. That's why I can't figure any one of those three in these murders, especially Milly's. Things were going too smoothly for them to risk any slip-up. There must be something bigger behind them then." He paused thoughtfully. "Um-m. Do you suppose the ten thousaand was a night's take or a week's? If one night then the Timbuctoo isn't the only customer they had."

Carton swore as he barely missed a confused pedestrian. "Incidentally, Joe, why has Van Pelt been so generous with loans to Dick? Or has Naomi Raleigh been seeing too many flickers?"

"No, she probably knew what she was talking about when she mentioned the loans to her uncle. That part isn't worrying me too much. Van Pelt is one of the trustees of that pile of dough and he's pretty sure of getting it back." He ran his hands through his hair. "What the hell! Cut out the questions, Kitch. I'm going nuts as it is. There isn't a thing to tie the murders to any of this stuff. Something screwy as hell is going on and damned if I'm not going to find out if I have to spend the rest of my life dodging the law."

They parked in the same spot back of Gloucester Tower and again used the stairs to May's apartment.

Kierney was asleep. May was playing solitaire. Goggles sat opposite, watching her fingers with unwinking absorption as she slid the cards onto the table. Joe put his hand on her shoulder and Goggles' eyes shifted there. He removed it.

"May, you were right," he announced. "Van Pelt and Martha Lane were at the Timbuctoo last night."

"I suppose they admitted it," she said, unimpressed.

"No, Puss denied it. I caught her before she could be convincing." He sat down. "And that's not all. Shasta and Wiener are clients of Van Pelt's. That ought to prove something."

May laid a red king in a vacant spot.

"It wouldn't be the first time a big time lawyer defended crooks, would it, Joey?"

"Of course not. That isn't what I mean. Van Pelt, the white-haired stooge of Park Avenue, goes to the Timbuctoo. The same night two people are bumped. One of them is his own client and left-handed member of said night club." He produced the bottle from Van Pelt's office. "And on my gum-shoe visit to the lion's den I find a bottle of the same stuff peddled by Shasta and Wiener. No. That ain't coincidence. It's a fairy story about the Big Bad Wolf." He put a black jack on a red queen. Kierney tossed the paper he had been reading to Joe.

"See what Miss Sands brought us, Joey. Them guys on the *Record's* giving us hell."

"I suppose they are." Joe opened the paper and let out a whistle. "Listen to this, Kitch." He folded the pages back and read the bulletin aloud.

NAOMI RALEIGH HELD FOR QUESTIONING

A new development in the Raleigh double murders arose today when it was learned that Naomi Raleigh, sister of the slain boy, was summoned by police for questioning. Her presence at a night club in company with Richard's party the evening of his murder was revealed as reason for her detention as a material witness. District Attorney Thaddeus Davy refused to comment further when questioned by reporters.

No trace has yet been found of Joe South and his companions, James Michael Kierney, former heavyweight contender, and David Kitchener Carton. Inquiries at a Times Square hotel where they were known to have been staying revealed only that the detective had checked out around five o'clock Monday evening.

Joe tossed the paper aside and shrugged.

"I'll be damned! So they've got angel-face in the can!"

May grinned. "You needn't try to look so indifferent just because I'm here. You may visit her *there*, too, you know. Not very cozy though," she added.

"Never mind that now," Carton protested. "It'll keep. Joey, give Miss Sands a swallow of that stuff you took from Van Pelt's office."

May looked up startled. The suggestion wasn't characteristic. Joe went to the kitchen and came back with a tray and four whisky glasses.

"What! No soda," Kierney said.

"No, smart guy," Joe reminded him. "This is what you call a tasting contest."

They sipped the whisky in silence. Kierney smacked his lips and reached for the bottle. "Where'd that come from?"

Nobody bothered to reply. Carton crossed his knees and filled his pipe. When he had it going he turned to Joe with a thoughtful frown.

"So they've finally got around to Social Register suspects. Van Pelt ought to be the next on their list. They must be getting desperate. Just another headache, Joe."

Joe said, "Trust her! She probably forced herself into Davy's office and they had to question her to get rid of her. I can just see the wench calling up the boys at the *Record* and practically dictating that item."

Kierney threw up his hands. "Geeze, Joey. Can'tcha talk plain United States? These murders got me goin' whoops now." He reached for the bottle. "Any more where this came from, Joey?"

"Plenty," Joe snapped. "But that's the least of my worries."

"Maybe we'll all be better off if we forget this business for the present," Carton drawled. He looked sidewise at Joe and reached for a book from the assortment on the table. "The police are still on the job and we are most effectively checkmated at the moment. I'm going to relax."

May shook her head and went into the bedroom. She returned almost immediately, pulling on the green slicker and carrying the hat box. Joe looked up then.

"Where do you think you're going, angel?"

"Oh, places." She shaped her hat before the full-length mirror on the door. "You don't think I enjoy sitting around here watching you three stiffs brood, do you? I'm going out and try to find some first-class sleuthing to do." Joe had risen and she pushed him back into the chair. "Take good care of Goggles and yon melancholy Dane. Murders or no murders, I'm a gal of action. In the meantime you might either make some attempt to figure it out or turn yourselves over to the police." She swung the hat box in front of Joe and struck a dramatic pose. The husky voice was mocking. "And remember, darling, whatever happens 'I must be cruel, only to be kind.'" She closed the door softly as she let herself into the hall.

The clock on the radio chimed once. It was four-thirty. Nearly twenty-four hours since Joe had met Dick Raleigh. He swung about restlessly. They would have to get a move on one way or another and see what was going on or they'd go nuts sitting around wondering.

"You two guys can sit here on your fundamentals if you want to," he growled. "But I'm the sucker that's on the spot and I'm going to do something, cops or no cops." He pulled the telephone toward him and gave the operator the number of the Hillman Hospital. When he had them on the line he asked for room 315. Raleigh himself answered. Joe said, "This is Police Headquarters. Is Lieutenant Murphy there?"

Raleigh said, "Lieutenant Murphy? The last of the police officers left ten minutes ago." Joe thanked him and hung up.

"Where are you going now?" Carton wanted to know as Joe slid into the reversible.

"I haven't reported to the old man since the first act. The old buzzard's got plenty under his fedora I'd like to know. Stick around and keep an eye on May in case the cops catch up with me."

Chapter Seven

THE HOUR HAND on the big clock between the two elevators pointed to one minute of five as Joe entered the hospital. He glanced hastily around. The girl at the information desk had her back to him. A white-haired woman who looked harassed enough to be a visitor stood in front of the elevator doors. Otherwise the place was deserted. The police were not in evidence. In the odd quiet Joe could hear a medley of distant sounds. The faint tap of typewriter keys; subdued murmurs; the low hum of business and suffering behind closed doors.

With no desire to advertise his presence he passed the information desk and walked quickly up the stairs. He turned right on the third floor and rapped cautiously on 315. When there was no answer he turned the knob and pushed the door in quietly. Raleigh was not on the bed. He hesitated and decided to wait. He glanced hastily around the room. It was just as he remembered it. Beside the bed on the medicine stand was a glass half-filled with water, a half-smoked package of cigarettes and an ashtray with two cigarette stubs and the remains of a cigar. The sick man had had other visitors today.

The door of the clothes closet was slightly ajar and Joe tiptoed toward it. He listened. When no sound came he slid cautiously inside. It was large and roomy. Two suits of clothes and a topcoat hung on the long rod and on the wide shelf was an expensive suitcase of the aeroplane type and a soft brown felt hat.

With bland disregard of ethics Joe went through the pockets of the topcoat. There was a pair of brown pigskin gloves in one, a handkerchief and two packets of paper matches. In another he found some change and an expensive powder compact. He grinned. The old man had ideas of his own. Joe removed the matches and slipped them in his vest pocket.

He was on the point of starting on the suits when he heard footsteps pause in the corridor and voices coming closer. One of them was Raleigh's. He said softly, "Nora, dear, I can't help worrying.

The police were considerate today, but they're not stupid. Sooner or later . . ."

Another voice broke in. It was Nora Gannon's, and the tones were soothing. "Now, Parker, will you let me worry about that? I'd rather lose my reputation than to have anything happen to you."

Raleigh's voice was tired.

"All right, my dear. But remember, you *can't* get mixed up in this business. You run along and let me try to straighten things out."

Joe heard the creak of the bed over Nora's low murmur and a second or two later the closing of a door. He eased the closet door open a crack. To his relief he saw that the screen would cover his exit. He waited a moment and slipped quickly across the floor and into the hall. This time his knock was answered by a startled, "Come in."

For a minute the look of cold fury on the older man's face stopped him. He said, "Good evening, Mr. Raleigh. I couldn't get here sooner."

Raleigh's tone was frigid. "Why are you here at all, South?"

Joe flushed and glared as he pushed the door to with his heel. Anger flooded him for a moment. He said, "Listen, Raleigh. I'm here to save for Joe South what your nephew couldn't save for himself. In this case it's mine. I'm talking about my neck." He clipped the last sentence with a gesture of his forefinger across his throat.

The Wall Street expression didn't flicker.

"Now that it's yours you're worried about it," Raleigh snapped. "I assume you mean to take better care of it than you took of Richard's."

Joe ignored that, waving it aside with one hand, and plumped angrily into the white chair.

"Cracks like that won't get us to first base. The police are on my tail and you know it."

A crooked smile touched Raleigh's lips.

"I know it. You know it, and seven million New Yorkers can't be wrong. Why did you do it, South?"

Joe started to rise, then decided to hold his ground. This time his voice was quieter.

"You don't believe that, Raleigh. Look." He leaned toward the handsome figure on the bed. "I haven't got time to sit here and play catch with accusations. You can think what you damned well please. I'm here because I'm in this thing up to my larynx, and I'm trying to climb out. Finding the killer is a hell of a sight more important to me than to you or anyone else. And I can't direct a search from the Tombs." He lifted a hand to halt Raleigh's attempted interruption.

"So let's cut the cracks. If I didn't want to see this thing through I'd be on my way to Mexico where they limit executions to election day. So let's start from the beginning."

He leaned back and put a cigarette in his mouth. He felt about in his pockets for matches and was about to strike one when he caught the name on the cover. It said "Timbuctoo." Dumbfounded he held the unlit match until Raleigh spoke.

"Exactly my idea, South." He leaned forward slightly. "Suppose *you* tell me what happened. Lieutenant Murphy was a trifle confused this morning, to put it mildly. He seemed to think I had you hidden in the hot-water bottle."

Joe didn't answer at once. His disconsolate gaze shifted to the window. Across the tops of the dirty tenements he scowled at the swirl of rain and wind and wished mightily for a drink. The case was getting screwier by the minute. He knew now where Raleigh and the nurse had been the night before. Yet everybody, including the press, believed him too ill to leave the hospital. His eyes returned to the bed. Raleigh was looking at him expectantly. "Well?" he prompted.

Joe struck the match and touched it to his cigarette. He put the packet back in his vest and looked straight at Raleigh.

"All right, you asked for it. Van Pelt gave me a job to do. It sounded like a goofy idea to me then. But if he wanted to humor a sick man and pay somebody to wipe the kid's nose I could play along with him. He knows I don't test high on ethics, but he knows very well I'm not a crook. I needed the dough, and I couldn't be choosy." He clamped his lips shut and frowned heavily.

Raleigh said, "I'm waiting."

Joe thumped the ashes angrily from his cigarette.

"Every time I think of what I let myself in for because that smooth Dutchman's mouth got a zipper on it I get mad as hell." He thrust a finger at the sick man. "And you didn't do any better."

Raleigh met Joe's angry eyes with a puzzled frown.

"Just what do you mean, South?" He looked genuinely perplexed. The man was either a darned good actor or a fool.

Joe said, "Do you mean to tell me, Raleigh, that you actually didn't know that Richard was the front and collector for a bunch of bootleggers?"

Raleigh's astonishment was genuine.

"Bootleggers, South? Are you crazy? This isn't the Prohibition era, you know!"

"It doesn't have to be. There's a type of mug who'd find a way to make a racket out of collecting flowers from potter's field. Figure it out for yourself. The law-abiding liquor dealer has a Federal and state tax added to the price of his stuff. Bootleggers fake labels on inferior whisky. They sell it for bonded brands, evade taxes and undersell the licensed dealer." He proceeded to explain Richard's tie-up with Shasta and Wiener. Raleigh listened with growing agitation. "And," Joe concluded, "I stuck my neck way out in the dark and got myself nearly killed last night." Briefly he related his adventures of the night before.

Raleigh found his voice. "You think then that these men are responsible for Dick's death?"

Joe looked at him a long moment before he answered.

"I don't know. According to last reports Naomi takes that honor."

Raleigh looked down his nose and said impatiently, "Yes, yes. I know all that. She called a few minutes ago."

"How's it affecting her?"

"Like anything affects her." The older man smiled. "She'd probably be thrilled under other circumstances." He glanced at Joe expecting him to understand.

Joe did. He said, "Why did they detain her in the first place? Routine questioning, or something more definite?"

Raleigh shrugged. "She says they're trying to get a line on all the people who were in Dick's party at the Timbuctoo Monday night. That would leave you and the Shermond boy. My personal opinion is that they're stymied and are just putting on a show for the benefit of the newspapers."

Joe watched the rain and wondered what he'd say next. Maybe he'd better take a flyer. He said, "Look here, Raleigh. Let's forget Naomi for the moment. You want me to be frank, don't you? I think there's something cooking a helluva lot more serious than Richard's would-be Al Capone complex. I've got to have cooperation. You're the only safe contact I have. So I'll have to give it to you as it comes." He paused to let that sink in.

Raleigh looked blank for a moment and said, "Keep talking."

"All right. Here it is. I believe Van Pelt is at the head of this racket." Raleigh didn't look blank now. He gasped like a fish that had got too close to the hook. Before he could speak Joe went on to outline his theories about Van Pelt's connection with Wiener and Shasta. He gave it to him with both barrels. "I don't know whether Dick was wise to Van Pelt or not. I'm working on it and what I find will either clear him of a hand in the murders or else. Knowing Van Pelt I can't see him murdering for a measly ten thousand dollars, let alone to keep out of the clutches of Mr. Hoover's Hawkshaws."

Raleigh hadn't missed a shot. He pulled himself to a sitting posture. His face was gray. He said uncomfortably, "South, I guess I owe you an apology. I've been accusing you of criminal neglect. You've made remarkable headway in spite of the handicaps. I appreciate it." It was the biggest concession he'd made and Joe took advantage of it. He didn't relax, however. There was still a touchy piece of business ahead. He took a packet of the matches from his pocket and laid them on the medicine stand.

"Mr. Raleigh, where did you get these?"

Anger flooded the sick man's face. He snapped, "That's none of your darned business, South." He looked as though he'd like to take a swing at Joe. The detective got up and stood over the bed.

"All right, Raleigh. It's your cow. But that's an example of what I'm up against. Go clam on me if you want to. You've thought you were pretty smart all along the line. Look what it's got you. I'm pretty good, but I can't work with one hand tied behind me and the other stroking your ruffled feathers. When you get ready to talk let me know. In the meantime, you might remember there's a murderer on the loose. If anything else happens don't hand me that stuff about white-eyeing on the job." He folded his arms and looked straight into the patient's eyes. "You've got a niece who is not only a potential heiress, but a very attractive one at that."

Raleigh's voice was still cold, but this time it held less rancor. "What are you expecting, South? Whatever it is, you were hired and paid to prevent what happened before. You've done a good job *since*, up to a point. But you've got to do a lot better to convince me that you have a right to ask too personal questions of me."

There was no trace of casual good humor in Joe's voice as he answered. His normally friendly eyes were steely. For the first time it occurred to Raleigh that Van Pelt hadn't been mistaken in his judgment.

"I don't give a cockeyed darn whose tender feelings I walk on," Joe snapped. "I'm out to find the murderer. I'm in a hell of a spot myself, and if it's going to take high-powered kicking around to get me off I'm going to do it. Remember that, Raleigh."

The sick man smiled for the first time in several minutes. "You know, South, I might like you in time."

"Well, don't try too hard."

"All right, forget the hard words," Raleigh said. "They won't change anything. What I'm concerned with now is getting this mess straightened out with a minimum of fuss. Do that, South, and my personal check for five thousand dollars will be waiting for you."

Joe's eyes brightened and this time his voice was completely without anger. "Now we're getting somewhere."

He reached for his hat. "I'm on my way. Just one thing more, Raleigh. Who gets Dick's share of the estate now that he's dead?"

The steel returned for a moment to Raleigh's lips. Then he shrugged. "It remains in the original trust fund, South, to be dispensed according to the terms of the will. Why?"

Joe looked at him sharply. Side-stepping again. He braced himself and plunged. "You wouldn't have access to all that dough, as trustee, now that Richard's dead, would you, Raleigh?"

The older man's eyes were like ice-cubes. His voice lashed at the detective like tempered steel. "What are you hinting at, South? There's a limit to what I'll take from you."

Joe tried hard to make the shrug casual. "Oh, just checking up," he replied with his hand on the door. Another thought struck him and he decided to risk it. "I'd better leave a telephone number where you can reach me." He scribbled May's telephone and apartment number on a card and placed it on the medicine stand, retrieving the Timbuctoo matches at the same time. "I don't suppose I need warn you not to let the police get hold of that card," he cautioned.

"Naturally." Raleigh hadn't seen the detective take the matches. He extended his hand. Surprised, Joe took it. At the door he turned. He said, "I'm wasting my breath, I guess, but just to keep the records straight, where were you last night?"

Raleigh stared haughtily. "Is there no limit to your impertinence, South?" he snapped. "It *is* wasting your breath and I'd advise you to get busy in other quarters if you hope to earn that five thousand."

Joe grinned. "I thought it wouldn't be any use, but I've got to keep in practice." That had hit the old boy. Before he could say anything more Joe slid into the hall and closed the door behind him.

In the lobby he hugged a pillar to avoid a plainclothes man who was getting into one of the elevators. He exited into the street as a cab pulled up at the hospital entrance. He made a dash for it. In the back seat a girl wearing dark glasses was counting change. Her hands trembled and she almost dropped some of the coins. Joe's glance shifted from the fingers to the glasses. Behind them he recognized Naomi Raleigh. He looked up and down the street and waited for her to get out. She wore the same slicker but the costume this time was black. The gamin grin was missing and she looked like a small, sad ghost.

Joe touched his hat. It worked. She whipped the glasses off and gasped, "Joe!" Her eyes were burning more than the normal amount of current and her face was coming to pieces. She tried to speak. The sound that came was like water washing oats down a horse's throat.

The detective said, "Take it easy now. You'll be okay in a minute. What you need is a shot." The muscles of her arm tensed. He guided her away from the hospital steps while the rain covered their retreat. The girl was still using her handkerchief to muffle hysterics. Joe looked for a bar. The self-appointed business of playing Galahad was getting awkward.

"This'll do." He pushed through a door on their right into an atmosphere of fried hamburgers and stale beer. The place was empty except for a sleepy bartender reading a tabloid with large black headlines. The man looked up with bored indifference as they found a booth away from the door. Joe helped Naomi shed the slicker and took the seat across from her. She had begun to get hold of herself and looked calmer. She said in a voice that still trembled, "You saved my life just now, Joe. I had to talk to somebody." She covered her face with her hands. "Oh, my goodness, I had to identify Dick."

Joe said, "Easy does it," as the sleepy bartender shuffled toward them. He ordered a double Scotch for himself and hot brandy for Naomi. Neither of them spoke again as they waited for their drinks. The girl's fit of trembling had returned and Joe was busy feeling sorry for her.

The waiter returned and set the drinks on the table. Naomi drank half the brandy in a gulp. Color came back to her cheeks. She said, as though she had just noticed Joe's presence, "Joe, have you seen the police yet?"

"I spent most of the afternoon with them," he lied.

She looked startled. "Then they aren't holding you!"

He didn't argue the logic of that. "Is there any reason why they should? How about you? How come you're on the loose?"

"Oh, you mean what you saw in the *Record?* That was just routine, Joe. They said it didn't mean a thing. In fact, they were very nice about it. But you. The papers said the police were looking for you."

"The papers *can* be wrong. The police have my alibi and appear to be satisfied with it. That meadow-dressing in the papers was just a gag to give the killer more rope." He looked at her speculatively. "But you'd better watch out. When Thaddeus Davy puts on his bedside manner with a pretty woman it's a signal for danger. I've seen him smile at them with his whole battery of dental work and the next day send them to perdition without a qualm."

59

Naomi's mouth started to crumple again. Joe pushed the remainder of the brandy toward her. "Here. No more of that. Finish your drink. I'm going to send you home."

She shuddered and swallowed the last of the brandy.

"Oh no, Joe! Not home. I want to go with you." The trembling had ceased and she was looking more normal.

Joe groaned. It was happening again. He leaned toward her and spoke with emphasis. "Now look, Naomi. I've got work to do and I can't do it with you tagging around after me. Not only that, but you've had all you can stand. How about forgetting the Girl Scout business for a few days?"

The gamin grin returned. She said, "But, Joe, I told you I don't want to go home. I'll be much better off with something to do, I know I can help you."

Joe swore. He said, "I thought you were on your way to see Uncle Parker when I ran into you. Why don't you go and see him? You'll do a lot less harm that way."

"But you said the police were there. I don't want to see any more police today."

Joe was impatient. "Well, you'll see plenty of them if you stick around me long enough." He added disgustedly, "What you need is a nice quiet spot to rest. If you're looking for excitement why don't you heckle the Red Cross to send you to England?"

She disregarded the last remark and concentrated on the first. She said excitedly, "Oh, so you're working with the police. Joe, how thrilling! Where are you going now?"

Joe had risen muttering curses into his whisky. He said, "What a helluva pest you turned out to be! And never mind where I'm going. Wherever it is you'll be headed in the opposite direction."

"Can't I even walk down the street with you?" She was pulling on the slicker.

"Walk! In this rain?" He pushed the door open.

Joe's desperation increased. He had looked forward to a trip to the warehouse in the hope of a lead. With Naomi in tow he was bound to get nowhere fast. The warehouse, he knew, was only a few blocks away. With rain washing their faces he headed in the opposite direction. It didn't work. Naomi was at his side matching stride for stride.

They had gone only a block when a cab pulled up at the curb and a familiar voice said, "Want a lift, Buddy?" It was Pete.

Joe said, "The bum penny. Can't I ever shake you, dope?"

Pete winked mysteriously. "I got dough invested in you, Joey. I ain't takin' no chances."

Joe said, "All right, all right. For once I'm glad to see you," and gave an address he hoped was a block behind the warehouse. He had taken careful note of the route the night before. To his disgust he saw that Naomi had already climbed into the rear seat. He shrugged resignedly and got in beside her.

He said, "Now look. I haven't time to take you home, but the driver will. In the meantime, you don't like the police to question you. All right. Maybe you'll like my brand better. Where did you and Shermond go last night after you left Harlem?"

Naomi's eyes crinkled. He thought she was going to say "Goody." He hoped she would. Instead she said, "We went home, Joe. That is, Charles took me home and left immediatetly. Does that make us suspects, Joe?"

"You mean to the Gramercy Park apartment? Where does Charles live?"

"He used to live in an attic on Christopher Street. Lately, I'm not sure, but I think he's living at that new place that's going up somewhere on Ninth Street. It's the Tomorrow Club, and he's doing the interior. He does murals," she added proudly.

"I'll have to get in touch with him right away," Joe reminded her. "Do you know the address?"

"Not exactly. But you can find it easily enough, I'm sure. May I go with you?"

"You may not. You're going home as soon as Pete drops me. By the way, what do *you* think about Shermond?"

"Me?" Naomi widened her eyes. "You mean in connection with the murders? Why, he hadn't even met Dick until about a week ago."

"And how long have you known him?"

"Six months or a little longer. I met him at one of those Greenwich jams. He interested me because he's different from the usual playboys I meet."

Joe said, "I can imagine."

"Don't be so superior, Joe. He's all right." She lowered her lashes. "You might as well know it now as later. We are engaged to be married."

Joe let out a a long breath and said, "Oh-h, I see." He looked at her expensive attire. He thought of Shermond's shabby sedan and frayed shirt cuffs and shrugged. Naomi, with her avid delight in the unusual, *would* pick up a stray like Shermond. "No," he said after the long pause, "I didn't realize that."

"Naomi grinned. "I could do worse, you know. Charles is really making a name for himself in murals and I'm sure I can help him."

"Great little helper," Joe murmured.

"Well, I can," Naomi insisted. "He may seem peculiar to you and Uncle Park, but he has a lot of pride I admire. He goes around practically starving himself and won't take a dime from me."

Darned peculiar, Joe thought.

Naomi said, "All right. Now please may I ask some questions? What happened to you last night?"

"I'm the little man who wasn't there," Joe growled. "I was drugged, dumped, found the body, was beaten, kicked and got my feet wet. Enough?"

"*You* found Dick's body?" Naomi gasped.

"No, I found Mildred Evans." He peered through the rain and tapped on the window. "Hey, Pete. You can turn here." He went back to Naomi. "I also got the dope on the gang Dick was working for."

Naomi's eyes opened wider. "You *do* work fast, Joe. Dick didn't tell you that, did he?"

"Of course he didn't. I got it from the big boys themselves. Last night at their warehouse. That is, where they keep most of their liquor."

"And do the police know all this?"

"Not unless they've caught up with Wiener and Shasta," Joe assured her. "Which I doubt. I guess I'll tell them myself this evening."

"Why didn't you tell them this morning?" Naomi insisted.

"Because, Bright Eyes, I don't tell everything I know to the police. And I've got a few jobs I don't want messed up. That's why I'm leaving you here." Joe tapped on the window again. "Pete, let me out near the alley. And see that you take Miss Raleigh home." He gave Pete the Gramercy Park address and slid out before Naomi could protest further.

The rain had let up a little as Joe came out of the alley and circled back on the parallel street where he expected to find the warehouse. A drug store on the corner reminded him he'd better do a little checking before he tackled the place. The store was deserted except for a clerk behind the fountain. Joe slid into a booth and called Van Pelt's office. He was surprised when Martha Lane answered. Working late. He filed the thought for future reference. He muffled his voice and asked for Mr. Wiener or Mr. Shasta. The accent said, "Just a minute," and a moment later, "Whom did you say, please?"

Joe pronounced both names carefully. The dignified tones slid back over the wire. "I'm sorry, we have no one here with those names. Who is calling, please?" Joe said, "Charlie McCarthy," and hung up. He felt sure the two men were there with Van Pelt, but he'd have to chance it anyway.

The rain had stopped for a breathing spell. Feeble sunshine cut a hole in the blanket of India ink clouds.

Joe found a bell beside the steel door and rang it three times. There was no response. He moved around into the alley where he remembered a side entrance. He was almost to the door when a figure loomed out of the mist. It said, "Joe," in a tense whisper. Joe swore in several octaves. He ended helplessly, "I'll break Pete's neck for this. How'd you get away from him?"

Naomi was triumphant. "Don't blame him, Joe. He knew all the sob stories and wouldn't budge. Between the rain and the traffic it was easy to slip out when he wasn't looking. And here I am."

"Yeah. There you are. And about as welcome as Goebbels in the Bronx. Now that you're here, for the luvva Mike keep quiet and keep your hands to yourself."

She said, "I'll be good, Joe."

Joe said, *"Will* you pipe down. This isn't a pink-tea party. I've got work to do." He pushed the bell beside the door. Again there was no answer. He remembered the keys which had been a part of Kierney's loot. He had to try most of them before he found one that worked. A moment later they were inside. Joe shouted "Hello" and the walls returned his greeting.

He touched Naomi's elbow and guided her toward the occupied section of the barnlike building. The interior looked like the inside of a cave, with its spider webs and air of desertion.

Two moving vans stood in the middle of the gloomy space. The cases which had lined the walls the evening before were nowhere in sight. He guessed they would be in the vans. They were. The place had a look of abandon. All set for a quick getaway. He stepped into what he supposed was the office and sniffed. Somebody had been smoking here recently. Joe tried to place the vaguely familiar aroma of pure Havana. He had smelled it just lately and under less pleasant circumstances. It came to him with a jolt. Van Pelt. He tried to figure that and gave it up.

He looked around. Naomi was tiptoeing about peering into dark corners. He supposed he ought to be grateful for her silence.

On a small, much-battered desk was a partly used roll of bandaging gauze, a bottle of iodine and a pair of scissors. Next to the scissors was an ashtray, with two cigarette butts and the long ash of a cigar. No doubt now. Van Pelt had paid a recent visit to his clients. Near by stood a small safe, its doors open. In another corner was a makeshift clothes closet. Its rack held several suits, a raincoat and a topcoat. Among them were the evening clothes Shasta and Wiener had worn the night before. Joe went through them. The pockets were empty. He carefully replaced the loot, including the money Kierney had taken. He fingered the material in the slightly overtailored dinner coat.

"Um-m, expensive tastes our boy friends have," he observed as Naomi moved to his side. She peered into the dark interior of the closet and ran light fingers over a rich tweed suit sized in the 50s. Joe grinned at her expression of amusement. She whispered, "What's in the vans, Joe?"

The detective's face brightened. "You give me an idea, Bright Eyes. Would you like a drink on our friends?"

Without waiting for an answer he went back to the trucks. The doors on the rear opened like an ambulance. To his satisfaction they were not locked. The cases were piled almost to the top and he had to climb up the sides to reach one. He had little difficulty getting it down. He succeeded in prying the top off with the tire tool. With the aid of his nail file the cork came out easily. Naomi, who was still tiptoeing curiously over the cement floor, came to his side. Joe handed her the bottle. "Ladies first," he said.

She grinned and tipped it to her lips. She looked at the label and handed it back to the detective.

"It's not bad, Joe."

"Not for bootleg stuff," Joe agreed taking a long drink.

"So that's what the racket is," she gave him the gypsy smile. "Clever."

"I'll say they're clever. But not clever enough this time."

Naomi looked at him thoughtfully. "You don't think *they* killed Dick, do you, Joe?"

"I wouldn't know, sister, but I'm going to find out." He took another swig and handed her the bottle. "Hold that while I put this stuff back." He returned the broken case to its place and swung the doors to. "Give me that. If I had room I'd make it two. As it is we'd better be getting out. They'll be hot-footing it here as soon as Beacon Hill can add two and two and come up with the right answer."

Naomi followed him to the door. As he started to open it a small sound caused him to glance at her. She was trying to repress a sob.

He said gruffly, "You've been pretty good so far. Cut that out now. I'm going to send you home where you belong."

"I'm sorry, Joe. I won't do it again. I hate to think of poor Dick and Uncle Park. Please take me with you."

They were in the street now and Joe closed the door behind him. The automatic lock clicked. He said patiently, "My dear girl, I can't take you with me everywhere I go. And right now I'm going home. Nothing exciting about that, is there?"

Naomi said, "All right, Joe. But promise to call me if anything happens." She fumbled in her purse and brought out a card on which a telephone number had been scribbled.

Joe was relieved. He slipped the card in his pocket and said, "Okay, I promise."

They walked nearly two blocks before they found a cab. For a wonder it was empty. For the second time Joe repeated the Gramercy Park address. Naomi raised her hand in friendly salute as the taxi swished away from the curb. He decided to walk the block east to Lexington Avenue Subway. He was so wet now a little more wouldn't make any difference.

Chapter Eight

KIERNEY opened the door to Joe's ring. He looked as though he'd been asleep all afternoon. Carton, lying on his back with Goggles on his chest, was singing a music hall ballad.

Kierney said, "Look. Kitch, the cops ain't got Joey yet."

"I didn't think they would, Mickey," Carton returned without missing a beat.

Joe grunted and disappeared into the bedroom. His garments clung to him with moldy discomfort. He put the bottle of liquor under May's pillow and peeled them off. The shower felt good. Through the hum of fine spray Carton's voice was low and melodious. Joe had never heard the words before, but the melody was sung with a lilt which reminded him of the feuding Hatfields and McCoys. It was the sad tale of a little English maiden who loved not too wisely but too well. He lowered the shower pressure to hear the words.

Joe heard the hall door close. There was a clapping of hands followed by May's voice.

"Wasn't that the *Lambeth Walk* you were singing?"

"The Lambeth street walker, you mean," Joe said through the door.

"Well, Number One Boy," May retorted as Joe emerged in one of her smocks, "whatever it was it sounds elegant when he sings it Come on out, Charlie Chan, and I'll buy you a drink."

"You'll what?" Joe went back and switched off the shower.

"I said come out and have a drink."

When he re-entered the room May was lifting a nearly full bottle of Scotch from the hat box. The three men watched curiously as she poured drinks and solemnly gestured for them to help themselves.

"Well, how is it?" she asked as Joe put his glass down.

"What's the gag, May?"

She pulled the hat box toward her without answering. In it were the two half-full bottles she'd taken away in the afternoon. She placed them on the table in front of the detective.

"You were right, Joey," she told him. "Both these are phonies and they come from the same keg. The drink you've just had is the real bonded stuff." She added firmly, "Which reminds me—you may add *that* little item to your expense account. It set me back the price of a good pair of pigskin gloves."

Joe noticed that though all three bottles looked identical, on each one a typewritten sticker had been pasted.

"It's good whatever it is," Kierney observed. He had another.

Joe's face looked like something lit up for Hallowe'en. He said "Come again. And in the meantime, what are these kindergarten cutouts doing on the bottles?"

May sat down. "I thought since you were merely speculating when you said those were faked labels I might as well check up and get proof. You may need it. When I saw how much Van Pelt's bottle resembled the ones Mickey got from the warehouse I had an idea. I took them down and had them analyzed and certified proof attached. They're both excellent phonies with counterfeit labels Wouldn't the F. B. I. boys like to know that?"

"I'll be damned!" was all Joe could say. Then he looked at her suspiciously. "And how do *you* rate access to an analyst, young lady?"

May got up and stood in front of him.

"You were damned a long time ago," she reminded him, "for being so stupid." In case it might interest you, I'm still aces high with that Columbia laboratory assistant you pretend to be so jealous of. *He* telephones twice a week, and this evening I accepted his dinner invitation. That analysis is the result, smarty."

She pushed one of the glasses toward Carton. The Englishman bowed, said, "Cheero," and poured the whisky slowly down his throat, savoring its excellent flavor. Joe scowled.

"This," Carton said simply, "is Scotch." Nobody contradicted him.

May switched on the radio. She said to Joe, "Did you find out anything helpful this afternoon?"

The detective recounted his visit to the hospital and his excursion to the warehouse with Naomi.

Kierney jumped. "Naomi? I thought they had her in the can."

Joe said, "They didn't put her in jail, dope. They merely had her up there for questioning. She said 'They were all very nice about it,'" he tried to mimic Naomi, "and they let her go."

Carton said, "What about Raleigh? Did you get anything from him?"

"Well, I discovered for one thing that he isn't as sick as he's supposed to be. He was out of the hospital last night." He told them about his eavesdropping in the clothes closet and the finding of the Timbuctoo matches. "I'd like to know what they were doing gadding about in the rain. They *could* have picked up the matches any time, but I wouldn't lay a bet they weren't at the Timbuctoo last night."

May sat down and drew her chair closer. Carton was stroking Goggles and watching May. He said, "Why didn't you ask him about it?"

"I did, and the old boy told me to mind my own business, but he obligingly supplied me with some new angles. For instance, Kitch. Dick's share of the estate stays where it is. At Raleigh and Van Pelt's mercy."

May said, "Oh, so? Didn't you say Richard and Milly were planning to be married this week, Joe?"

Joe didn't answer. He was thinking.

Carton said, "Um-m. Another point to ponder is how did the killer manage to get into the Raleigh house?"

"That's easy," Joe said thoughtfully. "All he had to do was to take Dick's keys. Whoever it was saw a light in Dick's room and had to investigate. Mildred Evans must have seen the whole thing from his window, turned on the light to get to the telephone, and was surprised there in the hall by the murderer. Her fingerprints on the upstairs extension suggests that theory."

"But I thought she was killed in bed," May put in.

"Milly probably fainted or was knocked out by the killer, who put her in bed and shot her while she was still out."

Carton reached in his pocket and brought out a wallet. From it he took a bill and folded it lengthwise. This he used for a baton, substituting the Siamese for an unseen orchestra. When the recording came to a close May switched to another station. The announcer said, "In exactly thirty seconds it will be seven-thirty."

Joe said, "There ought to be some news on now."

Carton unfolded the bill and studied it carefully. It was one Joe had given him the evening before. The detective finished inspecting the labels and watched absently as the announcer reviewed the latest war news and followed with local events.

"Another complication in the sensational double murders in the Raleigh case developed early this evening when the police raided the warehouse and headquarters of a gigantic bootleg ring in lower Manhattan. It was alleged that in addition to two truckloads of moonshine liquor bearing counterfeit labels police collected certain facts which prove a definite link between the slain boy and the bootleg racket.

"It was not known whether any arrests were made. The only other item of interest was the mention of Frankie Shasta and Hyman Wiener, prohibition barons, in connection with the raid.

"The police refused to comment further except to say that their lead came through an anonymous telephone call, and that they believed their informant to be a woman."

Joe said, "It's Naomi Raleigh. Who else could it be? And it certainly would be like her."

May smiled crookedly. "Why should she have made an *anonymous* call?"

"Probably," Joe reasoned, "because she didn't want to go into details. Besides, she thinks she's a second Mata Hari."

Carton pulled himself up and walked slowly across the room to the Scotch. He poured just a finger and lifted the glass to Joe.

"Examine that bill carefully," he suggested. Joe did. There seemed to be nothing extraordinary about it. He said so. Carton came over and pointed to the lower left-hand corner. There, in almost illegible green ink, in capital letters about a sixteenth of an inch high was the legend "R. S. V. P."

Joe produced the roll of bills from his vest pocket and together they examined the remainder of the currency. All bore the same legend.

"What do you suppose that means?"

May took the bills from his hand.

"You got them from Van Pelt, Joey. Do you think he would know?"

Joe didn't answer. He was trying to remember something about letters that had nothing to do with the English interpretation. He crossed the room and took a Bronx directory from the telephone stand. In it he found Van Pelt's home address in Westchester.

"It doesn't jell," he observed. "His initials are S. C., I remember now. His name is Stuyvesant Cecil."

May took the directory. She said, "Anyway, even if those were his initials why would he put them on this money?"

Joe was getting into the wet reversible.

"It isn't cricket. It's baseball and Van Pelt is Chance. Anyhow, I'm taking a chance on seeing Van Pelt."

May said, "The condition of your feet is going to your head. Out with it, flatfoot. Translate the double-talk."

Joe left without answering. At Grand Central he found a cab. The driver wasn't Pete. He greeted him without enthusiasm. The cabby said mournfully, "If this rain don't stop before midnight I'm gonna get me a launch. Whaddya think of the murders?"

"I think they're just dandy," Joe said brightly and gave Van Pelt's office address. He hoped he'd find him there. He dreaded a long ride to Westchester, but he was determined to see him as soon as possible.

He got out at 32nd and Fifth. The clock on the wall inside the lobby pointed to eight-twenty-five and he wondered if Beacon Hill would still be around. She wasn't. Van Pelt was seated at his desk reading tracts. Joe walked in unannounced.

"Good evening, Stuyvie," he said rudely.

"Oh, come in, Joe." The lawyer's voice was without emotion. "What did you do, walk up?" He studied Joe thoughtfully. "I understand you were here this afternoon."

The detective removed the reversible and relaxed in the armchair near the window.

"Yeah. I had a tea party with your squaw from Boston."

Van Pelt frowned. "If you mean Miss Lane, she didn't mention tea."

"Skip it." Joe settled back and grinned at the lawyer. "But I bet she did mention the Timbuctoo."

Van Pelt rose and turned his back on the detective. From the cabinet behind the desk he took a sealed bottle of Scotch. He said, "Nasty weather, isn't it?" He broke the seal and poured amber liquid into a tumbler. He handed the glass to Joe. Joe didn't drink it

"Not nearly as nasty as the tough sailing you're going to have when the cops get Wiener and Shasta in the can."

The lawyer lit a cigarette deliberately. "You mentioned the Timbuctoo," he said shortly.

"And you mentioned the weather," Joe reminded him.

The smoke ring drifted from Van Pelt's lips. "They're both nasty, aren't they?"

Joe lifted his glass. He took an experimental sip and smacked his lips.

"Do you get all your liquor from the Timbuctoo?"

"What little I use I get from Shasta." His voice was calm. "He has been my client for several years. Why?"

Joe tapped the bottle. "The rest of this is down in the police garage. I suppose you know that the warehouse was raided this evening?"

Van Pelt's voice was unctuous. "Joe, a lawyer's job is sometimes a difficult one. So far neither Frankie Shasta nor Hyman Wiener has surrendered to the police. When they do it will be my duty to defend them. I know those two men only as clients. The proprietors of a night club. I'm sorry to learn that they also traffic in illicit liquor."

Joe lit a cigarette. "Along with another of your clients?"

Van Pelt was definitely startled this time. "What do you mean?"

Joe grinned without humor. "That one on the slab," he snapped

The lawyer relaxed and sighed.

"That was the most disconcerting revelation of all. However, Richard Raleigh was not really a client. I was retained by his uncle, as you should know. The only other connection I had with him was co-trustee of his father's estate."

"It's a helluva set-up any way you look at it," Joe finally observed. "You hire me to protect a kid from a gang of hoods. They get him. Then you defend them." Joe was watching the lawyer closely, but his expression didn't change. He must be a good poker player, too.

"That's a quaint way of putting it, Joe. And not without an element of truth. As the saying goes: it's a vicious circle. A lawyer must eat."

Joe said, "Why?"

Van Pelt ignored that one.

"Your observations, however, have one notable discrepancy Neither Shasta nor Wiener had a finger in those killings."

"How do you know?"

"Because I have their word. I realize, of course, that in any crime truth becomes the first victim. But let me repeat, Shasta and Wiener did not commit those murders."

Joe reached for his coat and rubbed his stomach.

"Touching faith, but I'm afraid I can't share it. They nearly committed one last night down at their warehouse. Who do you think is guilty, Van Pelt?"

The lawyer knocked the ashes from his cigar and picked up the tracts. He didn't look up. "*They* think you are. Are you, Joe?"

Joe buttoned his coat. "Yeah, I'm a sex maniac. Didn't you know? Which reminds me, where did you and Bessie go after you left the Timbuctoo last night?"

For the first time Van Pelt's eyes changed expression. They were wary now and he smiled without mirth. "Joe, it's none of your darned business. We were not, however, as you may suppose, playing stump-the-leader on back alley fences."

"All right, maybe you can tell me something about this." He had taken out the roll of bills and now he handed one of them to Van Pelt. The lawyer looked at Joe and then at the bill.

"What's the matter with it? Counterfeit?"

"Look in the lower left-hand corner."

Van Pelt brought it closer to the light.

"R. S. V. P.," he murmured.

"Exactly. Know anything about it?"

Van Pelt shook his head. "It's beyond me. But wait. Do you have any more of these?"

Joe handed him the remainder of the roll.

"I'll be darned, Joe. What do you make of it? They couldn't have been stolen."

Joe was watching him intently. "Where did *you* get them, Van Pelt?"

"I?" The lawyer's astonishment was genuine. "Do you mean these are the ones I gave you?"

Joe said, "The same," and waited.

Van Pelt's eyes hardened. "It's none of your darned business, and I'd like to know what you have on your mind."

"Nothing, Stuyvie, absolutely nothing." He returned the bills to his pocket and added casually, "By the way, before I go I'd like to have some information about the status of the Raleigh estate now that Dick is dead?"

Van Pelt paused with his cigar halfway to his mouth. He shrugged "I'm not supposed to divulge these things, Joe. After all, I hired you and I'm the one to ask questions. But I suppose you are still working for me."

He eyed the detective with suspicion. "Or are you?" He didn't wait for Joe's answer. "Never mind. I'll get the file." He rose and went into the outer office carefully pulling the door behind him.

Joe slid back into the chair by the window. Now what? This was too easy. He had expected the old fox to protest, but here he was practically handing Joe something on a silver platter. Probably a nice sharp dagger to stick in his throat. Was the buzzing in his head due to the wind or had he had too much of Van Pelt's Scotch? His chin touching the edge of his collar brought him up with a jerk. Good heavens! He'd almost gone to sleep. For the first time he realized he was very tired. He tried to look brisk as the click of the opening door told him Van Pelt was returning.

The lawyer was carrying a thick file. He resumed his seat behind the desk and riffled through several pages. Presently he removed a legal looking document and gave Joe a calculating glance.

"I won't bore you with legal technicalities, Joe. You know how Dick's share was to have been disposed. If he had married, his widow would have inherited. As it is, it remains in the trust fund and reverts to Naomi."

Joe said, "Yeah. I heard that one. What about Naomi? I understand her share is pretty well tied up."

"Oh yes. I told you all that before. Her income now is the same as Dick's was. When she's thirty she will have full control of the money. If she marries before that her allowance will be increased substantially, but in any event she'll have to wait five years for the full amount because she's only twenty-five."

Joe said, "Pretty soft for you and Parker, huh?"

Van Pelt said between his teeth, "I don't like that."

Joe stared hard at him. "I didn't expect you would, Stuyvie. Dick didn't like that hole in his guts. Not much. I only meant that it's easier to shuffle a five-year trust and deal off a few extra greenbacks, than it is to give up the handling of two millions all at once."

The lawyer's lips made a triangle as they clenched downward. "Look here, Joe. You've been . . ."

Joe interrupted him. "Don't you put on act for me, chum. You take yourself too seriously. How does Raleigh feel about Naomi marrying Shermond?"

"Oh, he's opposed to it. I don't blame him much. The boy is a spineless dreamer, though he *is* beginning to be noticed in his field." He shuffled a page and went on thoughtfully. "Parker Raleigh's had his hands full with the two children. Richard's threat to marry the Evans girl may have been just that. I don't know. I do know he was quite capable of doing it." He sighed. "Since you are working for both of us, there's no harm telling you that the old man has been losing heavily on the Street lately, which is partly responsible for his breakdown."

Joe got up thoughtfully. "Yeah," he said as he moved to the door. "Too bad you got a tardy mark on that one. I could have used it sooner."

Van Pelt pushed the papers aside. There was a satisfied smile on his lips. "Is that all you want, Joe? I assure you you are welcome to any other information I can supply."

Joe said, "I bet," as he swung through the door.

On the street he realized his interview had netted him little. Van Pelt had given him a neat run-around. Joe was certain that his two prize clients had reported fully on their encounter with him the evening before. If his reasoning was right it would eliminate Shasta as the part that went over the fence last. Wiener was out. It was easier to picture Ferdinand the Bull romping home with the Maryland Hunt Cup than to imagine Wiener taking a fence. Besides, the man who did that was thin.

Joe snapped his fingers. Mr. Charles Emmett Shermond required investigation. He would find the Tomorrow Club. It wouldn't hurt to scout around for some local color on Shermond before he saw him. The best approach was to make the rounds of some of the pseudo-Bohemian Village hangouts.

He ducked into the subway whistling a few bars of the *Faerie Queene*. When he came up he was in the Village. During the short subway ride he decided to talk with Shasta and Wiener at the first opportunity. That is, if he could catch them before the police did.

On Tenth Street near the square Joe found the café he was looking for. Though early, the smoke-filled Archangel was already crowded.

Painted on the walls, gaunt, ill-shaped nudes loomed through the smoke-haze like sexless ghosts. Joe sat a table and ordered beer. Small groups of men and women chatted excitedly. He returned to his contemplation of the murals. When the beer came he ordered another. Glass in hand he walked over for a closer inspection of the nudes. A man and a girl joined him. The man, in a voice he thought at first coming from the girl, said, "Don't you think it's divine?"

Joe's control was perfect. He stepped back with a swish and peered under his hand for effect. He said with classic simplicity, "Love-ly, lo-ve-ly."

All three returned to Joe's table. The detective introduced himself as North. The man's name was Alcott. The girl's Mercedes. Joe wondered where she got it. The rings dangling from her ears were the size of pancakes. He ordered cocktails for the couple and another beer for himself. He said, "Who did it? The painting, I mean?"

Mercedes looked at him over the rim of her glass.

"DeBasim did it last year before he went to Russia. He was doing posters in Moscow the last we heard." She grinned. "Poor guy. He's probably a post in a Finnish snowdrift now." The Alcott boy looked pained. Joe chuckled but decided not to encourage the girl. He said, "I thought it might be one of Shermond's."

Alcott brightened. "Oh heavens, no! Shermond's a surrealist."

"You know him?" Joe's voice was casual.

Mercedes picked it up. She said, "Certainly. Everybody knows Shermond. He's famous around here. There's not much demand for his work, though. This country is too new to accept surrealism at its true value."

"What!" Joe exclaimed. "You mean there's no market for surrealism?"

"Not in murals," Mercedes told him seriously. "Isn't it too quaint? Poor Shermond barely manages to eat. The unfortunate boy picks up little odd jobs here and there. Right now he's decorating the new Tomorrow club." She smiled nastily. "Of course, if he marries that little Raleigh dame he'll be on easy street."

"Do you know Naomi Raleigh?" Joe asked absently.

"Not very well," she admitted reluctantly. "But she's around occasionally with Shermond."

"Isn't she an heiress, or something?" Alcott piped.

"Or something is right," Mercedes snapped. "You never know though with the mess her family's in. I've heard that the old man isn't as rich as he was. So maybe Naomi isn't such a hard little nut after all. I expect she does love Shermond. He's all right really, and it looks as if he's going places in a big way," she added generously.

Alcott was grinning. He said, "Don't mind Mercedes, North. She's jealous."

Mercedes shrugged and scowled into her drink. She said, "You ought to go around and see Shermond's work at the Tomorrow Club if you're interested, Mr. North. It's on Ninth Street below Sixth Avenue. It hasn't opened yet. I understand Shermond is staying there until the place opens. They'll probably take it off the bill."

Alcott and the girl had another cocktail and Joe paid the waiter He finished his beer and made his exit.

Chapter Nine

THE exterior of the Tomorrow Club looked like a Rube Goldberg version of Frank Lloyd Wright. The door frame was a gigantic eye. The eye must have been an afterthought. Everything else was modern enough to look like it was ready to take off in a hurry.

On the eye's pupil cast in relief was the torso of a woman. Joe pushed the bell button. Chimes sounded. For no reason at all Joe thought of Milly lying dead in Richard's bedroom. The whole pupil opened.

Shermond stood in the doorway looking startled. He said, "Oh, it's you, Mr. South. Come in."

When Joe crossed the threshold of the eye into the belly of the Tomorrow Club he felt the same as he had on a New Year's afternoon three years before when he had suddenly come to playing cribbage with a negro schizophrenic in a Bellevue psychopathic ward. He wanted to get out. He didn't. He hung to what might have been a huge hand with its palm up. The place had no walls. It was outside. It was not a café at all. He was standing in an expanse of translucent green desert. He said, "What the hell is this?"

Shermond sat down on an army cot. It was the only piece of furniture Joe could identify.

"It's the lighting." The artist gestured vaguely. "It confuses every one. Here, I'll fix it." He crossed to a concealed switch and the indirect lighting brightened. The floor melted into the wall, came to end on the horizon. The effect was achieved by convergent lines starting on the floor and continuing to a vanishing point toward the ceiling. At intervals along the lines, painted cleverly in photographic detail, were sections of human bodies. An arm here, a pair of breasts there. The anatomical studies grew smaller as they neared the peak and expertly blended shadows gave them optical dimension. Here and there along the human skyline were painted roses realistic enough to pick and wear in your lapel. On the horizon was a metronome. It was real. Its monotonous rhythm was like a file sawing at Joe's nerves. He brought his gaze back to focus on Shermond.

"It's the goldarndest place I ever saw. What the hell's it supposed to be?"

Shermond gestured toward the cot.

"That's incongruous, but you'll probably be more comfortable sitting on it." He moved toward the monstrous hand and relaxed in its palm. It looked silly, but Joe didn't feel like laughing. He said instead, "You haven't answered my question."

Shermond uncoiled an arm and ran long fingers through waves of hair that must drive women wild. His answer came with the air of a mystic addressing a cult. His mind was a million light miles away. He gazed into space. He said, "Mr. South, nothing is important but Time. Time is everything. It's yesterday, today and tomorrow. It's right now. It always has been and always will be."

Joe lit a cigarette before he spoke.

"Skip it, hophead, and tell me where you were last night."

Shermond stared into space. The metronome sounded like a milk horse tiptoeing on a hollow floor. Joe got up and stood in front of it. For a moment he thought of Cairo and the chambers of dead kings. Only the Sphinx was missing. Well, he could sympathize with her. He had plenty of unguessed riddles with none of the answers. He swore softly and turned back to the artist.

"Get this, screwball. Time is damned important. A helluva lot more important than you think. You'd better talk and talk fast. If not you're gonna be setting that pretty fanny of yours in another hand. The hand of the law. And when the hand of the law gooses you you're cooked." Joe punctuated the pun by pushing Shermond's nose. The boy didn't move. He said, "All that is irrelevant. Death is Life. Life is Death. They're both means to an end without an end. They're both Time."

Discouraged, Joe shrugged and returned to the cot. Shermond came out of it for a moment. He asked dazedly, "Why are you threatening me, Mr. South?"

"I didn't mean to threaten you, Shermond." The detective's voice was pleading. "I came here to find out where you were last night."

"You know where Naomi and I were most of last night, and I must say, intellectually, it was highly unprofitable." He paused and raised sleepy eyes to the horizon.

"I'm sorry we didn't talk about Time." Joe was sarcastic. "I don't know why we didn't. We had plenty of it. What I want to know is what you did after you left us?"

"I don't see the reason for all these questions, Mr. South, but since it seems to interest you so much I took Naomi to the Gramercy Park apartment."

"Then were did you go?" Joe snapped.

Shermond hesitated. "Why ... I ... I came here, of course. I'm staying here, you know."

"What time was it?"

"I don't really know. There's no clock here. I never carry a watch."

"Approximately what time did you come here this morning?"

"I would say about an hour after we left you."

"Can you prove it?"

"Why no, I don't believe I can. I was alone here."

"Now listen to me, pantywaist," Joe said sternly. "I have no license to kick you around trying to get you to talk. But the police have. And speaking of Time, you won't have much of it left. You'd better cook yourself up a hell of a swell alibi. The police have clocks and they use them. You can't bump a couple of guys off and then play whoops with a song and dance about Time."

No emotion stirred Shermond's eyes as he returned Joe's gaze. His voice was vague.

"Was someone killed? Is that what you mean by talking about the police?"

Joe groaned. "Was someone killed! Now I ask you. Don't tell me you don't read the papers, boy friend."

"I never touch them." Shermond shuddered. If he was acting, it was the best since Booth.

"Well, don't read them tonight, son," Joe warned. "Because they tell all about Mildred Evans and Richard Raleigh. How they were found in their own little round pools of blood."

It had no effect. Shermond's arm described another arc toward the horizon. Joe wondered what he would do when he could live with it no longer.

"They're both space. Death is space. So is life. They're both Time."

Joe's eyes studying Shermond's shabby clothes suddenly focused on the sleeve of his coat. It had a snag just below the elbow. A small piece of the tweed fabric had been torn away. He pointed to it now.

"You'd better get that mended," he said experimentally.

The artist touched it and grinned.

"Oh, that. I'd need a barrel first." For the first time his reaction was normal. "At the moment it's my only suit."

He accompanied Joe to the eye.

"Good night, Mr. South. Come again some evening and we'll discuss Time seriously."

Joe emerged from the pupil into Ninth Street without saying goodnight. He stood for a second welcoming the drizzle moistening his face.

"This," he addressed a lone fire plug, "is the cockeyedist case in history."

A few paces down the street he found a hamburger stand and had two hamburgers, while he thought longingly of the warm comfort of May's apartment. His second cup of black coffee he sipped more slowly as he tried to sort out the jig-saw pattern he had collected. None of it made sense. He tried to visualize Shermond leaping anywhere. But Shermond, if not actually the man who had tumbled over the fence, was a plausible possibility. Whichever way he looked, though, he couldn't fit a motive to him. But could he? He was engaged to Naomi and the girl would eventually have a generous income. He shook his head. That was screwy, too. Shermond wouldn't have had to kill anybody to marry the girl. He'd better see Naomi again while his visit with the artist was fresh in his mind.

He was still wondering as he sipped the last of his coffee whether Shermond was as innocent as he acted or whether he was taking Joe for a convenient boat ride up time and the river. He tossed a half-dollar on the counter and left the stand. He walked through Washington Square and up Fifth to 14th Street. There he turned right. Union Square was a swamp. He rode the Lexington Avenue local to 18th Street. He checked the address on Gramercy Park with the card Naomi had given him. The suite number was 31. He climbed the stairs instead of waiting for the self-operating elevator. There was no answer to his ring. He rang again. A moment later light footsteps approached. A cautious voice asked who was there. Joe had no desire to broadcast his name. He said, "It's the gentleman from Montana."

Naomi caught on and let him in.

She said, "Joe! This is wonderful. I thought you'd forgotten me."

He winced. She led him to a larger room decorated in classic modern.

Joe said, "Did I interrupt something?"

She flicked ashes into a crystal tray.

"Of course not. I was just going to shower. I'm going crazy doing nothing." She slid the bathing cap off. The mass of tumbled dark hair made her look young and appealing.

Joe sat down on a love seat that was half Duncan Phyfe, half World's Fair 1940.

"I've just come from Shermond," he announced without preliminary. "I thought I'd better talk with you again."

Naomi took another long pull. She sat down in the one-passenger mate to Joe's love seat and crossed her legs before she spoke.

"Oh, so you found him. Is he at the Tomorrow Club?"

Joe nodded. "Right where you thought he'd be. He's decorating the place and using it as headquarters."

"Isn't it a grand name, Joe? So original."

"He's an original man."

Joe grimaced. "You must like Time."

"Or *Life*, or *Fortune*, or *True Love Stories*." She grinned. "So you talked about his pet theory, did you?"

"He did. Not me."

"Yes, he would. He has some queer ideas. That is, queer to most people. I think I understand him. But just wait. He's going to make a name for himself yet."

A blast of wind shrieked against the window. Naomi got up and moved to the davenport. Joe shivered and went over to sit beside her.

"I suppose you realize Shermond's alibi for last night isn't worth a whoop in hell." He let the words sink in.

She moved closer. The housecoat rustled. Joe recognized the signs.

"Surely, Joe, you don't suspect Charles?" Her voice was husky.

"That," Joe replied, "is exactly what I came here to discuss."

She drew away from him. "Then that means you do."

"He has no alibi."

Naomi looked sideways at him. "Just what did he say?"

Her knee was pressing against him. It felt hot. He shifted his position.

"He says he went directly to the Tomorrow Club after dropping you here."

Naomi slid closer and snuggled against him. She smelled like violets and Joe wanted to put his arms around her. He didn't. He said instead, "I'm not Marc Antony, kid. *I* came here to talk. How about you listening?"

She raised her face and he saw that she was smiling.

"Afraid, Joe?"

His reaction was divided. He didn't know whether to kiss her or smack her. The slick satin housecoat skidded smoothly from under his grip and the arms snaked up and around his neck. It was all there was between Joe and Naomi, and she was still inside. She kissed him twice on half-parted lips.

The detective responded. He whispered into the ear under his lips. "This could be fun. But love ain't love with the cops on your tail. We were talking about Shermond. Remember." Firmly he loosened her hold. He got up and walked to the window. He stood watching the fury of the tempest outside while he tried to control the one inside. When he returned the girl's eyes were closed and she was lying relaxed on the soft.

"Okay, kid. The curtain's down on that act. How about taking time out to get back to the boy friend. You know. The guy you're going to marry?"

She struggled to a sitting posture and looked at him strangely. The current in her eyes was over charged. It came to Joe with a jolt. He said, looking at her steadily. "Better let up on the fancy needle, kid. Pretty soon your brakes won't work."

If he'd expected to startle her he was disappointed. She grinned, unperturbed.

"You don't miss much, do you, Joe?" She leaned back and stretched like a sleepy kitten. "Don't scold me. I'm so darned bored. I wouldn't need those heavenly little powders if you'd give me enough attention, darling."

Joe relaxed. Maybe it hadn't gone too far. He felt sorry for her. No harm giving the kid a lift.

"I'll remember that, sugar. I'm not Shermond and I don't talk Time, but I'm an artist. When all the wrinkles in this case are ironed out you'll be seeing more of Mrs. South's little Joey than Mrs. South herself. That's a promise."

Naomi gave the grin full throttle. Her eyes were accepting a mental promissory note.

Joe said, "Okay?"

He moved back to the love seat. "Now that our pleasant little affair has been shelved for future reference I can use this as a seat again. So back to Charles. What time, for example, did he leave here last night?"

She sighed. "Must we talk about it, Joe? You're wasting your time on him."

Joe wanted to know why.

"Because you are. Charles Shermond never did anything violent in his life. Besides he didn't have any reason to want Dick out of the way."

"That's what I'm trying to find out. People don't murder other people every day of their lives, but Shermond has plenty of reason to start framing an alibi."

"Do you think the police will arrest him?" Her eyes were excited again.

"Naturally. Unless he can tell a more reasonable story than he told me."

She got up and went to the window.

She said hesitantly, "Has it occurred to you, Joe, that if Charles hasn't an alibi for last night I haven't either?"

Joe said, "I hadn't thought about it. What are you trying to do? Stir up more trouble?"

"You have a right to think that," she said seriously. "But I'm honestly trying to help you now. It's important that Charles and I have an alibi, isn't it?"

He nodded.

"Then if the police believe me why couldn't they believe Charles?"

"It's possible that they don't believe you. I *know* Shermond isn't telling the truth. If I know it the police will know it."

"How do you know I told the truth?"

Joe studied her silently. "What's the gag?"

Naomi lit a fresh cigarette from the stub between her fingers. Her hands shook a little.

"You see it's this way, Joe. I don't mind the police suspecting me, but I couldn't stand it if Charles were arrested."

She'd thrive on arrest, Joe thought. He contemplated her with increased respect. "He wouldn't like doing time, eh?" He couldn't resist the pun. She ignored it and her eyes were troubled.

"Charles has an alibi. He wouldn't use it unless I made him."

Recalling Shermond's ignorance of what was going on outside his screwball set-up on Ninth Street, the detective wondered at her trust.

"And the alibi . . . ?" he insisted.

Naomi's reply was brief. "Charles didn't go home last night. He spent it with me."

"Good heavens!" Joe got up and went to the fireplace. He was sorry for Naomi. The crazy, courageous little wench. She had bought herself a peck of trouble this time. He said into the fire, "That's a tough break, Naomi. I hope for your sake you won't need to use that kind of alibi."

"I probably won't need it, but what about Charles?"

"If he talks to the police as he did to me they'll never know what hit them."

"I'm afraid they will."

Something in her voice made Joe whirl around and stare at her. Her hands were not quite steady as she dusted ashes in a tray. "Why?" he snapped.

"Because of a complication. When Charles left this morning there was a parking ticket on his car. The police are bound to check that some time."

"That is tough," Joe agreed. "But maybe they won't yet. They aren't on to him and Homicide and Traffic don't cooperate that well."

"We were going to get married soon. But now . . ." She muffled a sob. "I wish I were dead."

Joe was impatient. He snapped. "This is no time for melodrama, kid. It don't become you. Dry your eyes and sit tight. I'll have this case wrapped and tied with blue ribbon before the cops make their first hit," he added, with a confidence he didn't feel.

The girl didn't answer. Joe got his hat. "Did you tip off the police about the warehouse this afternoon?"

She nodded.

"I can't blame you much. But why didn't you tell them you were with me?"

She dabbed at her eyes and got up to adjust a log on the fire.

"I knew you weren't telling the truth when you said you'd seen them this morning. I knew they were still looking for you. I saw Uncle Stuyvie this afternoon. I was afraid I'd give you away if I told them it was I who was calling."

"Uncle Stuyvie? Oh, you mean Van Pelt?" Joe looked at her thoughtfully. "So you were up there this afternoon. All right, you win. Thanks just the same. Whatever your purpose it was a break for me." He shrugged. "This is the darndest case. If something doesn't break soon I'm going to confess myself. I'm sick of looking for the law behind every hydrant."

Naomi came over and stood beside him. The violets hit him again.

She thrust out her hand. "Friends?" she asked.

He took it. Her fingers were unexpectedly firm.

"More than that," he agreed. He paused uncertainly, said good-night abruptly and swung down the hall.

He left the building cautiously scanning the street. Hot tongs clutched at his eyes. Sleep. Some long-bearded guy had said something about sleep sewing up raveled sleeves. Well, he wished it would unravel some of the knots in this screwy case.

He boarded the subway with the grinning riddles still playing hopscotch over his brain cells.

Chapter Ten

MAY WAS AT THE RADIO when he opened the door. The voice from the radio was announcing ten forty-five. May switched it off and turned as Joe entered.

"You can stop sneaking about like a Hallowe'en witch at Christmas. Also it will be safe now to telephone Lieutenant Murphy and ask him to lunch tomorrow, on accounta they've caught the killers."

"They got Wiener and Shasta in the can," Kierney piped.

Joe didn't answer, but went on into the bathroom. A few minutes later he returned. He slumped onto the davenport without removing his soaked topcoat, too weary to express anything more than disgust.

"Okay. Let's have it."

May did the talking. She sat down next to Joe.

"The news just came through over the radio. They picked the boys up as they were getting ready to leave the warehouse when it was raided this evening. Apparently Wiener and Shasta were on the verge of moving their stock to a new hide-out. When the police searched them at headquarters they found young Raleigh's keyring among other interesting things. They put a bit of extra pressure on the arm and hammer boys and got them to admit they were in suspicious proximity to the murder house last night."

Joe said, "I could have told the police they had been around there last night."

"But you didn't," May reminded him. "You and the police, I understand, aren't on speaking terms."

Joe got up and removed his coat. The whisky was nowhere in sight. He took off his shoes and stretched out on the floor.

"If I weren't so tired," he announced to the room, "I'd go out and get plastered. That's the easiest five thousand bucks anybody ever lost."

May got up and stood over him.

"What was that, Robin Hood?" she inquired sweetly.

Joe rolled over on his stomach and covered his face with his hands.

"A mere detail I probably neglected to mention. Parker Raleigh made the offer. For uncovering the killer, of course."

Carton raised himself on an elbow and narrowed his eyes at Joe.

"When did all this happen, matey?" he inquired.

"And we suspected them gorillas all the time," Kierney mourned.

Joe sat up suddenly. "What was that news report again?" he asked excitedly. Carton repeated it.

"Wow! That one almost got by me." Joe was on his feet now.

"Most of them do." May interrupted rudely. "What's it this time?"

"Quiet, will you?" Joe was impatient. "I'm trying to concentrate. They can keep those two hoods in the jug and slap the cover on, but five grand ain't peanuts. Listen, Shasta didn't know Dick was dead when they gave me the business last night. But that don't cut no ice with the police. I know he wasn't acting. Why should he have gone into his act for me? Nnh-unh. All he wanted was that money." He sat down on the sofa with his hands locked around his knees.

"All that may be true, but the fact remains the money is still missing," Carton reminded him. "And a nice Harvard accent just said over the radio that the police still think you have it. They've that much in common with Frankie." His look was speculative. "You haven't it, by any chance, have you, matey?"

Joe stroked his unshaven chin thoughtfully.

"Cut the cracks, Kitch," he snapped. "No, I haven't got it now, but I'm going to. Listen, I talked with Van Pelt this afternoon. He's trying to put me off Shasta and Wiener. That's okay by me. Besides they're in the can. But I think I know why. Van Pelt, unless this rain's soaked through my skull, is more than their lawyer. If he isn't the brains behind that bootleg ring I'm a jackass. He was in that warehouse this afternoon before I got there. Someone ought to tell him to stop laying smoke screens with pure Havana. Furthermore," Joe continued, "he went pretty far off the main road to explain about how the Raleigh estate is divided. He says the old man's been losing his pants on the market. He's not being exactly subtle in trying to put Parker in the suspect lineup. I'll admit he's got an agle there. People old Parker's age don't get out of sick-beds to do the town in weather like this." The detective got up and took a turn around the room. "Incidentally," he mused, "Van Pelt didn't bat an eye when I flashed the marked bills. Got him worried, though."

"You think that means he's not responsible for the markings?" Carton observed.

"Precisely. The guy who did that—"

May said, "Van Pelt. V. P." She grabbed Joe's arm. "Look. How's this: Raleigh, Shasta, Van Pelt? R. S. V. P.?"

Joe looked at her admiringly. "Right smack on the old button, Babe." He turned to Kierney, ignoring Carton. "Remember the old double-play combination? Tinkers to Evers to Chance? Only it's the double cross in this game. The guy who started it wound up on the slab. Now here's the set-up. At least the way I have it doped. Don't ask me how he did it, but Dick Raleigh got wise to Van Pelt's interest in the fake hootch racket. Van Pelt, remember, is a stuffed shirt who probably gave him plenty of boloney about the integrity of a trustee and that kind of meadow-dressing. Raleigh wants money and plenty of it. He approaches Van Pelt for another loan. Van Pelt —foolishly, of course—cracks down on him. What is the dear boy thinking of—coming to him without his uncle's knowledge? Dick gets his belly full and ties up with Shasta and Wiener as ambassador of good will for the company without Van Pelt's knowledge. When he's in solid, and the sales chart starts climbing he goes to Van Pelt again. This time he connects—and why not? He's got Stuyvie where there ain't so much hair. Marking the bills was only incidental. It was probably something he meant to come through with if the old boy tried to shut him off. In short, blackmail, and pretty small potatoes for a guy who's coming into all that folding money. Cockeyed, maybe, but a heel's a heel on Park Avenue or Broadway."

Carton looked thoughtful. "That rather puts Van Pelt on a spot, eh?" he drawled.

"So much for Richard," May put in. "What I'd like to know is where Naomi comes by the wherewithal to wear emeralds and Schiaparelli nightgowns on two thousand a year. That's what her allowance is, too, isn't it, Joey?"

"That's what I said. But don't let it upset you. Anybody who wears nightgowns can get emeralds if they know what to do with them —the nightgowns, I mean. And they don't have to be Schiaparelli."

"Oh!" May looked at him suspiciously. "So Mr. South burned his mouth."

"Don't be feeble—say, what the hell are you talking about?"

"Oh, shut up," May snapped. "I suppose she got you all tied up in knots, Joey."

Joe patted her hand.

"Baby, the knots you've got me tied in would puzzle a bluejacket. Now keep still and don't be jealous or papa spank."

"Jealous!" May's voice was full of scorn.

"What else did you learn, Joe?" Carton stopped the by-play.

"I learned that Time is today and tomorrow and yesterday and life and death; in fact, everything but Time. I found out that all nuts are not in Bellevue; that a metronome is conical-shaped and that Shermond actually spent the night with Naomi last night."

Carton whistled. May said, "The poor kid."

"Yeah," Joe agreed. "I was sorry for her, too. She got a bad break there. But she loves the guy. She's got nerve. What make it worse is that there was a parking ticket on Shermond's car the next morning." Joe was suddenly still. He snapped his fingers. "I've got a hunch, Kitch. If it's right I'll still get a whack at that five thousand bucks." He reached for his coat.

May was at his heels. She grabbed his arm. "Now where do you think you're going? A minute or two won't make any difference. You're already soaked through and I bet the only thing you've eaten is a hamburger."

"Two," Joe snapped with his hand on the door knob. "Right now I'm more interested in another whack at old Raleigh. It's time . . ." He was interrupted by the telephone.

"That," said May reaching for the receiver, "is probably one of New York's finest."

It wasn't. Someone asked if Joe South was there. May looked at Joe and cooed into the mouthpiece, "Mr. South hasn't been here for three weeks." She listened a moment and turned to the Siamese with her hand over the transmitter. "This party wants to know where Joe South can be reached."

Carton asked who was calling. Joe moved closer and put his ear to the receiver. May said, "Who's calling, please?"

A high nervous voice threaded over the wire.

"If you should hear from Mr. South soon please tell him to call Tomorrow."

May said, "Call who tomorrow?"

Joe grabbed the telephone.

"Hello, hello, Shermond? This is South."

The voice receded into a sigh, came back. "Oh, Mr. South. Yes, this is Shermond. I got your number from Mr. Raleigh at the hospital. There's something I wanted to tell you about last night. It's been bothering me. I've just seen the papers."

Joe interrupted impatiently. "I know. You're going to tell me you spent the . . ."

Shermond cut in, "Yes, but . . ."

"Never mind that now," the detective snapped. "Stay where you are. I'm on my way."

He was hanging up when the instrument suddenly barked—then barked again. It wasn't Shermond—it wasn't a faulty telephone. It took powder and lead to do it. Joe looked at the receiver stupidly. He gasped excitedly, "Hello, hello!" He jiggled the instrument. There was no response. The click of the receiver at the other end had cut the connection.

Carton was on his feet. He looked as calm and dangerous as a post-Chamberlain Britisher. Gone was the weary indifference. His shoulders tensed. Joe turned to May.

"While there's five thousand bucks there's hope. Let's get going." He motioned to Carton. "Come on, Raffles, you're going to operate on an eye."

Carton was English. He said, "Damned clever of you to deduce where he was shot, Joe. I'm not a doctor, you know."

They found Pete parked at the rear entrance on First Avenue Joe punched him gently on the chin.

"Do you just hang around for a chance to badger me about that chicken feed? And, by the way"—he looked at the driver suspiciously —"how did you trace me?"

Pete leered and shifted into second.

"Oh, I get around. You ain't the only dick on the beat. Besides I got to look after my interests, ain't I?"

"All right, get us down to Ninth Street in ten minutes and I'll give you twenty bucks bonus for the missus."

Rain and traffic slowed Pete and it was a good twenty minutes before he pulled up at the corner of Ninth Street and Sixth Avenue Joe and Carton walked the remaining distance to the Tomorrow Club The street was almost deserted.

Carton was fascinated by the building. He walked into the street to get a better view. He said, "You Americans!"

Joe didn't hear him. The chimes sounded lonely. There was no response.

Carton took a bunch of keys from his pocket. A moment later they were inside.

Shermond's sprawled body was no surprise. It was what they expected. He was lying face down between two of the convergent lines The widening pool of blood was thick enough to float a dory. Joe stooped over the body.

Carton was studying the interior. He said, "Whoever did this must have been to Soho. It's a good imitation of Les Temps."

"Whoever did it did a thorough jub," Joe mused, still looking at the body.

Carton moved closer. Joe knelt beside the recumbent figure and examined it carefully. "The body's still warm," he observed.

Carton shook his head. "I wager you find some marked bills lying around." He paused as Joe let out an exclamation. "What is it, Joe?

Found something?"

Joe had ceased his examination and was scratching his head in puzzlement.

"Something wrong with the feel of the place." He stood up and peered around the walls. He pointed to the metronome. "That's it. The darned thing's stopped."

They both gazed at the pyramid-shaped instrument on the wall. Light glinted on its glass cover. Its inverted tongue was like a frozen death leer. In the eerie lighting a nightmarish chill crawled along their spines. Rain tapping the sidewalk made Joe think of the fall of dirt on a lowered coffin. He said, "Gosh, what a place, Kitch!"

"Quite!" The Englishman's voice was grim. "I bounced into a shell-hole once where a Hymie had just had his guts blown to hell. Rain filled the spot where they'd been and the bloke was asking for water." He brushed his hand across his eyes. "I hate to remember the quality of my laughter."

"Yeah. Save that for Hallowe'en." Joe shook himself. "Let's get moving. Wonder what stopped that gadget."

He pulled the army cot in front of the metronome and felt around its base.

"Uh-uh, here's one of the slugs. Darned good shot or just luck? Didn't even crack the glass." He peered closer and put a finger up to the outside base. "Yeah. Here's where she lodged. Gimme your knife." The slug was almost completely embedded in the hard wood and it took Joe a minute or two to pry it out. He rolled it in his hand and handed it to Carton. "That may come in handy, pal." Carton examined it carefully and returned it to the detective.

"I'm no ballistics expert, but that looks like a .32 to me."

"Sure. They's beginning to whistle to me in my sleep—when I sleep." He stepped from the cot and bent over the body again.

Carton came and stood beside him. He watched with interested curiosity while the detective began a systematic inspection. From the dead boy's pockets he removed a packet of newspaper clippings, mostly about the progress of his work. He flipped through them and returned them to the pockets.

The wallet which he found inside of Shermond's coat was good, but old and well-worn. There was nothing unusual in the ordinary identification cards and the stub of a ticket to a year-old Art League ball. He glanced closely at the parking ticket, dated that morning with the time scribbled below the formal summons. It said six A. M. In the money section there was a single hundred-dollar bill. Joe whistled and turned it over a couple of times.

"For a guy supposed to be flat on his fanny this stiff was well-heeled. Where do you suppose he got that?"

"Bonus from the killer, perhaps," Carton replied. "When it didn't work he used a bullet. He probably left it to mark another red-herring for the police, or he might even have forgotten it in his haste."

Joe put the bill in an envelope, scribbled his initials on it and handed it to Carton.

"There, hang on to that. We might need it."

Carton took the envelope, removed the bill and examined it more closely in the suffused light.

"Look, Joey," he pointed to the lower left-hand corner. "That man's here again."

Joe looked and let out a stream of invectives. "I'm getting darned tired of that R. S. V. P. stuff, It's . . ." He broke off in the middle of the sentence. He said tensely, "Do you realize the significance of this?"

"Exactly," Carton agreed. "You're getting too close for comfort, Joe."

"And this is only the beginning. I've still got ideas," the detective snapped and started toward the exit.

Carton replaced the bill in the envelope.

"I say, Joe," he paused uncertainly beside the body. "What about this johnnie? We can't just leave him here, you know."

"Oh, can't we? Wouldn't we look ducky toting it around town. Watch this." He lifted the receiver off by the cord, and with a handkerchief over his forefinger dialed a Spring number. When he heard the first signal connection he dropped the instrument and left it dangling. He reached over and pushed the light switch.

Carton followed him through the exit and closed the weird contrivance that passed for a door. The heavens started another torrential downpour and water beat their faces as the detective looked up and down the street for the cab. Pete had moved a block further away from the club. The two men started to sprint toward him when Carton, with his hat pulled lower over his eyes, collided with a buxom figure wrestling with a large black umbrella.

"I beg your pardon, madame," he murmured as he moved out of her way.

She let out a full-bodied oath, glared at him and trekked unbeautifully down the street, the umbrella fluttering about her ears like a huge black crow.

"Tough oats," Joe growled as he pulled Carton after him. "Whose job is the worst—ours or the charwoman's? Let's hope she's as short on memory as she is on looks."

Pete was chewing tobacco and adding a column of figures when Joe opened the cab door. The detective took the pencil away and put it in Pete's pocket. He said, "Put away the slide rule, Euclid, and get this crate rolling."

The driver spat viciously and let in the clutch.

"Never a dull moment," he groaned. "I don't make nothin', but I can't complain about the ringside seat, Joey. Now I ask you, pal, is this the way to treat a pal?"

"Skip it, dope. Get moving or we'll all be eating out of tin plates. Find a dark spot to telephone. First place you come to."

Pete passed a Broadway bus with his hand out and said over his shoulder, "Geeze, Joey, this ain't no fun."

The cab had turned at a side street and slowed in front of a drug store lit like lovers' lane. Joe jumped out and told Carton to wait. He pushed the door open. A little bald-headed man with a stoop and a gray druggist's coat came around the counter.

"Just closing," he greeted Joe as though it was too much to expect a paying customer at that hour. The heavy voice had a Teutonic flavour.

"All right, pop. I want to use your phone."

He slipped into the single booth and leafed the directory till he found Van Pelt's home number. The buzzing signal continued for several seconds before the instrument at the other end was lifted. Joe almost dropped the receiver when Martha Lane's too-sweet voice gurgled over the wire.

"Listen, my little chickadee, get Van Pelt on the wire right away if he's there. He's going to take a fast IQ, and I mean fast." A suspicious sound drummed Joe's ear. There was a pause and the secretary said, "Those other men scooped you, Mr. Fields. He's engaged . . ."

Joe got it before she was cut off and a gruff masculine voice cracked impatiently, "All right, what is it, buddy?"

Joe tucked away his first favorable thought of Martha Lane as he replaced the receiver and crossed the floor in two strides. He slid into the back seat and spoke to Joe through the glass partition.

"Get going, pal, the bloodhounds are on the scent and the ice is melting fast. Don't ask questions. See how much distance you can put between us and that pillbox station in the next ten minutes." He was breathing hard as he turned to Carton. "The blue shirts are sure goose-stepping in this parade. Darn funny hour for them to call on Van Pelt. Martha Lane's there, too. Shermond was right about time. I could use a little right now."

Carton's voice was calm. "Don't get excited, Joe. We'll go back to Gloucester Tower until they lose scent."

"Nuts to that. The way the GPU is clicking I'd be about as safe in May's apartment as Churchill in the Reichstag."

"That bad?"

"That bad and worse. Look, you go back to May's apartment. No." The detective lifted a hand to halt Carton's protest. "Don't argue. If the boys turn up be dumb and keep talking. I've got an idea and Pete'll be around if I need him. If my alley goes blind up against the eight ball I'll contact you somehow."

Carton shrugged. "Righto. But I still think you're balmy." He peered into the weather and tapped the window. "This'll do," he directed. Pete slowed, idling the engine. Carton got out and thrust a hand through the lowered window. He said, "Happy landings," and strode into the rain.

Joe was low enough to crawl under a snake's belly. Impotent anger and impatience met and exploded into classic profanity. Pete's voice sliced through a choice run.

"Hey, Joey, the marines can do better than that." He was bored and sleepy. "Where you wanna go now?"

The engine still idled. They had stopped in front of a dingy bar What Joe could see of the clock in the window said one-thirty.

"First, I want to tie a load on—let's get soused."

"Aw, Joey, this ain't no time to stop for a drink. Ain't it wet enough out here? Besides you know I don't go for that stuff. Do you suppose they'd have Moxie here?" he added hopefully.

"I don't know whether they got Moxie or Adolph," Joe snapped "But they have a telephone and enough Scotch to do the trick."

A moment later they pushed thankfully into the steam-clouded tavern. Pete followed to the rear where they found a booth for two.

The pock-marked waiter who took their order had a face like a wire photo. His nails looked like he'd been digging in a subway. He said, "Some night, gentlemen. What'll it be, gentlemen?"

Joe didn't look up. "Uh-huh. Swell night for a murder. It'll be a double Scotch for this gentleman and a bottle of Moxie across the table." He gestured toward Pete. "You said Moxie, didn't you, pal?"

Pete nodded. "I said Moxie." He looked sleepy.

The detective found Naomi's number scribbled on a rain-smeared card. With the first signal the receiver was lifted. She must have been standing right beside the instrument. Maybe she was waiting for a late date. Her voice was wide awake as she repeated the number with formal efficiency.

Joe said, "This is South, kid." There was a pause and then, "Oh yes. Hold the wire a moment." In the pause that followed a faint rustling noise slivered over the wire followed by a quick, "Yes, Joe?"

"I'd like to see you . . ." Joe began and broke off when the noise became an undertone of masculine voices. One of them said, "Keep him talking."

Gently the detective rehung the receiver. Pete was dozing over his empty glass when Joe dropped a bill on the table.

"Another fade-out," he said with the corner of his mouth. "It's the cossacks again." Pete rose mumbling, but he was ahead of Joe when they reached the street. Outside they made a dash for the cab. Pete slammed the door, now wholly awake. In three seconds flat they were off on the side street and into Broadway.

"The cops have all the cards this hand," Joe said tersely. "They'll have that dump looking like a policeman's ball in five minutes. I bet there were enough cops in Naomi's apartment to fill *Esquire* with gags for a year."

Fiftieth Street loomed ahead on Broadway. Joe's eyes brooded unhappily at the rivulets of water splashing the gutters and thought again of the Missouri farm. The times they'd prayed for rain. Right now he'd like to be stranded with the mirages on Mojave. He slid forward and spoke to Pete over the back of the seat. "Keep moving until I can think of something, chum." His voice was worried.

Pete's sigh exploded with disgust.

"Hell, Joey! Are you gonna keep this up all night? I got to sleep some time, ain't I?"

Joe said, "I thought you were my pal, pal."

Pete swung left at 52nd Street. A police scout-car skidded to a stop next to the cab as a red light went on at Eighth Avenue. The driver swore and Joe slid further down into the rear seat. As the car shot forward again he quoted dolefully, " 'Brethes there a man with soul so dead.' " He started to sympathize with the guy who made it famous and decided to feel sorry for himself instead.

"Joe," Pete spoke for the first time in several seconds, "I can get you some Scotch, but it'll be worse'n the cops."

"Anything," Joe sneezed. "Anything to dynamite this ice jam in my belly."

They turned left on 30th Street with the green light. A block further on the car shaved the curb and stopped. Pete got out. He didn't look at Joe, but said without moving his lips, "Duck, Joey, the cops," as three policemen spilled out of the grease-smeared door of a tavern on their right.

The detective dropped to the floor, resting his back against the seat. Pete was inside the tavern before the uniformed men reached the police car a half dozen steps down the street.

Joe closed his eyes. Fatigue picked crazy swing on his nerves. The growl of fog horns joined the rhythm and the rain on the roof jitterbugged to the goofy melody. Pete's hand on his shoulder brought him out of it.

"Hey, Joey. Wake up. Here's your fire-water."

Joe's eyes were dazed. He scrambled back on the seat and reached for the uncorked bottle. Some of the liquid slushed over as the cab jerked away from the curb. The detective didn't wait. He tipped the liquor and drank deeply.

Pete drove downtown on Seventh Avenue. At West 14th traffic tangled and he swore again. No police were in sight. As the cab shot forward at Greenwich Avenue Joe said, "Do you have to play prima donna with this bus? How about a little less limelight?"

A clock in the window of a Western Union office said two thirty-five. Before they reached Christopher, Pete turned into a dark side street and slowed. Joe tipped the bottle again. He leaned against the leather back, the liquor cradled in his arm like a baby. Exhaustion shut his eyes. Now he was in a boat. It rocked and a clock ticked. Out of the fog Shermond's face took shape, framed by a smoky halo. Corpses dotted the distance between the face and the horizon. The dead artist's mouth clicked open and shut in time with the clock. He was trying to speak. Joe couldn't understand. No sound now but the clicking of the dead boy's teeth—that and the rain. The meaningless code switched to Morse as Shermond and halo fused into Pete's back and the code into the cab's meter. Joe came to with a jolt which almost upset the whisky.

The cab had stopped. Joe said, "What's the matter now?"

Pete's face wore the weary, pathetic look of a bloodhound. "We ain't got much gas left, Joey."

"Where are we now?"

"Battery Place," Pete answered mournfully. "You been asleep, Joey?"

"Oh-h-h, no," the detective said disgustedly and tipped the bottle to his lips. "I've been playing Freud. Wasn't it wet enough uptown, dope? Or did you bring me down here to sleep with the rest of the fish?"

"Aw, Joey," Pete scratched his head helplessly. "Ain'tcha had enough? It's three-thirty. How much longer you gonna suck on that bottle?"

Joe said, "Ha!" and took another drink. The driver pressed the starter sadly and nosed the cab toward Trinity Place.

Joe had reached the halfway mark on the bottle and his head felt like a tennis ball; love all, sixth set.

The driver shouted above the wind, "You won't need much change outa that hunnerd now, Joey. It'll be cheaper to give you the hack."

Joe drained another two inches from the bottle.

"Stop heckling me about small potatoes. You'll get your dough. Think of me flushing five grand down the drain. If I had half the money you and Shasta think I have I'd be on the beach at Bali enjoying sunshine and grass skirts instead of playing hide-and-seek through the gutters of New York." He lifted the bottle again. "Cripes, this is lousy stuff!" The liquor was reaching low tide.

The cab lurched as Pete shoved on the brakes for a police ambulance. The wind was so high now he hadn't heard the siren. An exclamation from Joe made him turn. The jar had spilled the remainder of the Scotch.

Pete said, "Geeze, Joey. Pipe down, willya? I got enough troubles now. My crate's gonna smell like Chatham Square with that liquor all over it."

The detective didn't answer. He was now busy fighting off the nudes from the Tomorrow Club. They were all trying to dance with him, and Shermond's face with its mouth open grinned with macabre glee. His eyes were bloodshot and heavy. He wished May would let him go to sleep. She was reminding him of something important. His body felt like slow-motion looks. He shook his head. He was very drunk. Suddenly all the disjointed shots of the crazy kaleidoscope dissembled to a far wall. Then with the exactness of Music Hall Rockettes they formed into lines of military precision. Van Pelt's office stepped smartly into place. Martha Lane and the Beacon Hill accent took on shape. Nora Gannon and Parker Raleigh; Hillman Hospital, the Harlem dive and Dick and Milly dancing. One moment they twisted in snaky mist; the next they cleared and the picture was complete.

The scene in the Harlem restaurant moved to the front, and through a fog he heard the last words between Richard and Milly before the Mickey Finn took its toll. "Great watch-dog—our pal— the boys at three o'clock—passed out on a half-dozen drinks—passed out—passed out—passed out—a half-dozen drinks."

The chill that clutched Joe's spine brought him upright and cleared his mind. What a blundering, cock-eyed ass! That fixed it. If he were right, the case was as good as closed right now. Elation nearly sobered him. The next moment he groaned. There was still a vital piece of evidence he needed.

"Five thousand bucks!" he shouted.

Pete pulled to the curb. He shouted back, "Cut it out, Joey! Remember that crazy nigger you . . ."

Joe laughed aloud and the driver cut the engine. He looked around then as if he were afraid of what he'd see.

Joe said, "What time is it?"

"Time to quit this foolishness." Pete's voice was persuasive. "It's nearly four o'clock, Joey, and you're drunk. *Now* what crazy idea hits you?"

"Never mind that," Joe said impatiently. "Sometimes I'm so

dumb I could play Dopey dwarf without rehearsing. Where can I find a telephone?" He laughed again. "Boy, I don't even need a directory for *this* one."

Pete glanced back once pityingly and slushed into the dripping traffic again.

The storm which for nearly three days had beaten and flooded Manhattan reached its fury around four o'clock. Figuratively and literally it kicked New York into a cocked hat, and brought wrinkles to the unlined cheeks of Mr. Valentine's newest rookies. Dollars and doughnuts poured into the pockets of hundreds of New York taxi drivers, including Pete, who waited at the wheel of his cab while his fare dialed a familiar telephone number, which didn't answer. and, aided by the storm's roar, broke down a door to satisfy a hunch.

When Joe finally joined Pete he was carrying a pigskin brief case. He snapped curt orders and Pete wasn't far behind. He did things to the car's mechanics and it moved swiftly through distorted streets. Joe smiled grimly and relaxed. At last he was headed for the goal line with the pigskin tucked safely under his arm.

Chapter Eleven

CARTON stood at the window in May's apartment frowning into the sheets of gray water slapping the panes. May paced the floor from window to radio and back again. Kierney had found an old copy of *Vogue* and mooned sadly over silk-stockinged fashion photographs.

None of them had thought of sleep. Carton had turned up at a quarter of two with the news that Joe was still a length ahead of the police. He had given them a stamp-size account of the finding of Shermond's body, but had been unable to reassure them further

After that, conversation lagged. May interrupted the pacing and paused beside him. Her eyes were clouded. She said, "You shouldn't have left him, Mr. Carton. If he gets near one mahogany bar he'll end up with a lot of steel ones."

Carton's smile was bleak but it was an effort.

"He can take care of himself, Miss Sands," he comforted her.

She didn't answer. The housecoat rustled as she moved to the radio and turned the knob. A swing band wailed into the room and she switched hastily to another station. The impersonal voice wading out with the latest news bulletins chilled her.

". . . Lieutenant Murphy of the Homicide Bureau, who made preliminary investigations, said circumstances indicated that Shermond had been murdered. No motive was given. The promising young muralist was well known in New York art circles, and friends said . . ."

May's lips tightened and she switched the knob viciously. She said, "The big goon. He might as well turn himself over after this. It's all Murphy's been waiting for since that kidnaping case. This covers the well."

Kierney said, "They ain't wastin' no time."

Carton made a clucking sound. "You don't know Pete. He could hide a rhinoceros in Columbus Circle. They'll have to catch Joe first, you know." He turned from the window to watch May. He said. "Joe's been in tighter spots, Miss Sands. No use getting upset."

May crossed the floor and relaxed sidewise on the davenport with her knees drawn up under the housecoat. She twisted her head and looked at Carton with blue, sleepless eyes. The smile she gave him was her substitute for tears. She said, "That crazy lug isn't worth thinking about."

A blast of wind whipped into the room and the door bell rang.

Kierney leaped from his chair, spilling *Vogue* and the silk-sheened legs to the floor. May came to with a start and Goggles, her back arched, trotted to the door.

"Joe," May breathed, her face brightening. Carton saw that she was as alert as though she had not been dozing for the last half hour

"More likely the police," he observed as the bell rang again.

"I'll slap 'em down," Kierney grunted and started for the door.

"All right, Charlie McCarthy," Carton stopped him. "I'll handle this. Pipe down and keep quiet."

He opened the door. A lank man stood there with a hand raised to push the button again. His eyes were gun-metal agates. He wore a heavy slicker and his hat was pulled low over his eyes. Behind him two hefty men in uniform scowled at Carton. They were both fat and one of them had a broken nose.

Carton saw that the tall man wore plainclothes under the slicker. He pushed his hat back and looked at the Englishman with somber interest.

"The Limey, by gosh," he greeted him. "I didn't expect to see you."

"How are you, Lieutenant Murphy?" Carton returned pleasantly. "We haven't met in some time, have we? Won't you come in?" He moved away from the door and bowed.

"No," the Lieutenant's voice was cold. "I'm looking for a murderer. Joe South, to be exact. Is he here?"

"I'm really sorry we can't oblige, old man, but Mr. South has moved and left no address. Won't you come in and have a drink?"

May had risen. She looked at agate eyes and back to Kierney.

"Mickey, make these gentlemen some coffee," she ordered. "They're all wet."

"Geeze, May, do I hafta?" Kierney complained.

"We ain't here for a party," growled broken nose.

"Pipe down, Fritz," Murphy snapped. "We might as well be comfortable. Looks like we'll be here for a while. There's a few questions I want to ask these people," he added with heavy sarcasm. "I know the palooka there, Carton. Who's the dame?"

"The *lady* is Miss Sands," Carton's voice was icy. "Please remember it."

"All right, all right," the policeman apologized. "I'm sorry, lady, but these mugs pick up strange females." He looked around suspiciously. "Mind if we give the place the once over?"

"Not at all," May said sweetly. "But the pent houses here are much more attractive. Sun-porch, potted plants, a full view of the river . . ."

Broken nose said, "Sun porch! In this weather?"

The other policeman said, "She thinks that's funny."

Murphy said, "Cut the cracks and keep an eye peeled," and disappeared into the bedroom.

Suddenly Fritz grabbed Kierney by the arm. He was staring fascinated at the bottom of May's skirt. "My gosh," he gasped. "Do you see what I see?"

May looked down. Goggles' head was poking from under the edge of the housecoat. For the first time in several hours she threw back her head and trilled a laugh that started at her toes and came all the way up.

"Didn't you ever see a Siamese cat?" She finally found her voice.

Fritz' face looked as if the photographer had just told him to watch for the birdie. He let out a breath he'd been holding. "Cat! Geeze! Did you hear that, Max?" He shook his head. "A cat!"

Goggles trotted to him and rubbed against his trousers. Fritz looked pleased and picked her up as Lieutenant Murphy emerged from the bedroom. He looked suspiciously at the tableau. "What's the joke?" he growled. Nobody spoke, but Fritz dropped Goggles like a hot coal. She gave him a reproachful glance. The lieutenant pulled a fragile rocking chair forward and sat with his legs around the back.

The detective gazed around the room like a fighter watching for an opening. Kierney leaned against the kitchenette door, a contemptuous sneer on his lips. Carton watched the rain and hummed under his breath. May's smile was angelic as she met the lieutenant's glance with wide-eyed innocence. The two uniformed men stood awkwardly waiting for orders.

"Okay, time's up," Murphy suddenly snapped. "Now I want some straight answers. Where's Joe South? Don't try to tell me he hasn't been here. Shasta's stooge, Toni Siana, saw him coming here. Also that red-headed model at Fravessi's said he was a friend of Miss Sands'. Oh, no," he held up his hand as May started to speak. "We walked her into it. She didn't know she was shooting her mouth off." His chuckle was nearly human. "If you could have heard her when she found out I was a policeman you'd forgive her. You model gals get around."

Carton frowned. "All right, Murphy, get on with it."

"I asked you a question," the detective snapped. "Where is he?"

"I wouldn't know," Carton drawled. "The last time I saw him he was getting classically blotto. By this time he's probably sleeping it off in the park."

Murphy smiled without humor and tossed a folded newspaper to Carton.

"Ve-e-ery funny. Read that, wise guy, and you'll change your mind."

Carton flipped the paper open. Across the top he saw what he had expected.

THIRD GUN MURDER STIRS
MANHATTAN

Slain Artist Was Engaged to Naomi Raleigh

Search for Missing Detective Intensified

One of the most extensive man hunts in criminal history was intensified this morning with the discovery of New York's third gun murder in less than forty-eight hours.

Latest victim to the rapidly mounting list of cold-blooded killings was Charles Emmett Shermond, noted artist, whose body, severed from life by a single bullet, was found early.

"Oh, my gosh!" May gasped.

Lieutenant Murphy had been watching all three under sleepy lids. He said casually, "Maybe you'd like to do some talking now, Carton. What were *you* doing at the Tomorrow Club at one o'clock this morning?"

Carton's eyes were thoughtful as he glanced up from the paper. "I beg your pardon?"

Fritz doubled a fist and started toward him.

"Listen, Limey, we got a witness . . ."

The lieutenant stopped him with a glare. Fritz sat down grumbling. Murphy said, "I'm running this show, Fritz. I'll do the talking."

He got up and stood in front of May. He said, "Miss Sands, I don't seem to be getting anywhere with these mugs. Maybe you can tell me something. I'm asking you straight. Do you know where Joe South is?"

May's voice was flat. "I give you my word, Lieutenant Murphy, I'm as anxious to know where he is as you are." Carton knew she wasn't lying.

"All right, how about you, Kierney? And don't tell me any fairy stories about how you knocked out Bitsy McNeill. I lost ten bucks on you in that fight."

Kierney lounged away from the door and stood in front of the detective. He put a hand up to stifle a yawn. "Geeze, Looy, I ain't seen Joey since he borrowed a ten spot last Christmas. Wonder how the old boy's gettin' along."

"All right, fellah, so you're playing dumb. I've given you all a fair chance. No wonder the Commissioner can't get any action. Everybody's mouth's tied up with a zipper and the zipper's stuck. Here we are with eight million people sitting around on their fannies waiting for these murders to break and you lugs stand there and yawn in my face." He glowered at them. "I've given you all a fair chance and I can't get any co-operation. I wish you could see my side of it. Since you can't, or won't, I'll have to arrest Carton." He motioned to Fritz. "Bring out the bracelets and let's get going."

Fritz grinned happily. "I been waitin' for this break three years," he gloated and started toward the Englishman.

The detective looked at Carton who was smiling crookedly. "Carton, I'm sorry," he said. "I don't hold with your kind meddling in police business, but I know you try to be fair. In this case, however, you've lied to me." He sounded as though it were a personal affront. "You were really seen coming out of that screwy joint with a man whose description fits Joe South. We've got the woman who saw you."

Carton didn't answer. The policeman looked really sorry. Kierney glared. "What you think you're doin'? That wasn't . . ."

Carton stopped him. "Easy, Mickey."

The detective ignored Kierney. "I'm not arresting him on a homicide rap, but as a material witness. He's concealing evidence and the charge will stick." He turned to May. "I'll have to ask you and Kierney to come along too, Miss Sands. Of course, you'll be within your rights to refuse but I think it would be better for all concerned."

"Certainly, Lieutenant Murphy." Her voice was cold. "But we know, don't we, that what you're actually doing is making a big play. The papers are riding you because you haven't been able to put your hands on Joe South, and you think by arresting a whole flock of people you'll get them to change their tune. All right." She paused to let her words sink in, and her eyes flashed fire. "Get your gosh darn, evil-smelling flat feet out of my apartment, and I'll go with you to hasten the process. But let me tell you this. I wager you that this case will be closed in less than twenty-four hours and it won't be you that closes it." She turned and swept out of the room before anger could spill over into tears.

Early morning stillness hovered through the corridor as they closed the door behind them. Carton felt as though he were walking the "last mile" to his execution. The next play was in Joe's hands. He had done all he could, and if Joe's crazy hunch didn't click they'd find themselves looking at the rain through bars in another few hours.

Two police cars were parked in the rear. Murphy ordered Carton and Kierney into the front car and left May to join the two uniformed men in the other. A moment later they were off, their sirens mingling with the dull moan of fog-horns and the storm's monotonous dirge

Chapter Twelve

NAOMI RALEIGH AWOKE. Her head was heavy and her eyes were like sand. Drowsily she wondered what time it was. She rubbed her eyes. It didn't help and she pulled herself halfway up in the bed. Then she remembered.

She was in her own room. When the police had left the Gramercy Park apartment to follow the lead left by Joe's telephone call, she decided to go back to the 78th Street house. Hurriedly she had thrown together a few things and reached home soon after two. Unaccustomed fatigue with the hollow silence of the big house merged into regret for the whim which had prompted the move. Sleep was empty years away. Shadows played halting fantasies on her nerves. Dick's face on the slab; Mildred Evans whispering strange warnings. Time twisted back and queer trills cut through the labored moan of the elements like a funeral dirge. The girl shuddered, pushed the covers back and swung her feet to the floor. It was the door bell.

She felt for the light over her bed, switched it on and looked at her wrist watch. Three-thirty. She sighed and rubbed her eyes again. Her bare feet slid into the mules on the floor and she pulled on a heavy quilted robe. As she reached the hall the chimes sounded again. Panic clutched and angered her. She swore softly and tiptoed hastily back to the night stand beside the bed. From the drawer she removed a neat, shining little automatic and slipped it into one of the roomy pockets of the robe. She wasn't afraid, she told herself, but nobody was going to take her by surprise.

This time she didn't wait for another ring. She snapped the hall switch and the next moment she was speeding down the stairs to the front door. Relief flowed through her as she recognized Nora Gannon. It was reflected in the nurse's voice when she spoke.

"Naomi!" she gasped. "We thought Lamb would be here!"

Naomi withdrew from the open door pulling the nurse with her. She said breathlessly, "Gosh, I've never been so glad to see anybody in my life. And I'm glad it's you. Another five minutes in this house alone would have driven me mad." Then questioningly, "What made you come at this hour? Is Uncle Park worse?"

The nurse shook her head. "No, thank heavens that's not it. But being with the police hasn't improved him any. He's been with them since they found Shermond's body. . . ."

"Shermond. Shermond's body." It wasn't an exclamation. In a voice totally devoid of expression she stood dazed, repeating the name meaninglessly. Nora Gannon knew the signs. She pushed her gently back into the room.

A petulant voice stopped them. "Nora, who's there?"

Nora called "Coming," and turned back into the rain. Her progress to the door with Raleigh was slow and they were nearly drenched when they reached its shelter.

Naomi was sitting upright staring blankly at the opposite wall. Nora helped the sick man out of his coat and settled him in a chair near the fireplace. Then she returned to the girl.

"I'm terribly sorry, child. It hadn't occurred to me that you might not have known. And," she added, "so many dreadful things are happening, I had forgotten how close to Charles you were." Naomi didn't reply. She sat rigidly staring into space.

Parker Raleigh grasped the situation in a glance. He said curtly, "Nora, my dear, you'll find brandy in the dining room." Then he moved slowly and sat down beside his niece.

"My dear, dear child. Please pull yourself together. It's not easy, I know, this coming on top of Richard's death. It's a tremendous blow. But you've got to take it and you must be brave."

The nurse came with the brandy and filled three small glasses. She looked smart the way some nurses don't, in her navy blue suit and high heel pumps. The dark hair was parted in the middle and combed into a grandmother's knot on her neck. It suited her.

Naomi sipped the brandy abstractedly. Color returned slowly to her pale cheeks. Without seeming to open her lips she said haltingly, "Charles. Poor, gentle Charles." She drained the glass. "He was so kind. So very, very kind."

Nora Gannon knelt and put a match to the logs in the fireplace. Efficiency operated with every movement. The fire burned slowly, slashing shadows, turning objects into cowled dwarfs.

Parker Raleigh was facing his niece. She raised her head and tried bravely to smile.

"And poor Uncle Park. They can't even leave you alone. The police, I mean."

The gray-haired man grunted. "It isn't only the police. After all, it's their duty." His teeth clicked shut. "It's South again," he snapped. "When I get so completely taken in by a good-for-nothing four-flusher I have no one to blame but myself." He poured another brandy and handed it to Naomi.

Nora Gannon watched the girl finish the drink. Then she settled her gently back into the chair.

"Sit quietly for a minute, dear, and then you must go to bed."

Naomi looked at her blankly like a sleep-walker.

Raleigh was poking at the logs and watching the sparks with a heavy frown. Nora started to say something, but instead she poured two glasses of brandy and handed one to the sick man. She didn't speak until she'd settled herself on the ottoman by his chair.

"Do you suppose they'll get Joe South?" She tried to make the question casual.

Raleigh stirred the fire unnecessarily. It was a moment before he answered.

"Can't tell," he said shortly. "That depends largely on which way the wind blows—for South, of course. If he's still in New York he'll be found sooner or later. If he's not . . . well . . ." he broke off and handed Nora a folded newspaper from his coat. "Read that. It's the latest. I don't know much more myself. When the police open their mouths it's only to ask questions."

A blurred photograph, several times removed from the original negative, showed Shermond already looking like a cadaver. Beside it was an unflattering half-tone of a round-faced man whom the nurse recognized immediately as Joe South. Above them in scare headlines, she read:

POLICE OF FIVE STATES
SEEK PRIVATE DETECTIVE
IN VILLAGE KILLING

Nora finished the brandy and grinned wryly. "Forty-three more to go unless they've added Hawaii. Then there's always Mexico—or Brooklyn."

Raleigh poked the fire. "Somehow I don't think so. South's no mental giant, but the police aren't either."

The girl pulled the ottoman nearer Raleigh. He was silent as she read the item aloud.

"Then you *do* think it was Joe South?"

The question sounded empty. Nora hadn't asked it—neither had Raleigh. They both looked up startled. Naomi's eyes were shining like twin headlights, but she wasn't seeing anything. She was sitting rigidly upright clutching at the edge of the padded cushion. She added monotonously, "It's silly suspecting Joe: Silly."

The nurse moved quickly. She was by the girl's side in an instant. She pried the hands loose. They were icy cold. She said with brutal calm, "Snap out of it, Naomi. We know it's silly, but you must try to pull yourself together. You haven't been asleep tonight, I'll bet. We'll be taking you to the hospital next."

Naomi said, "Joe wouldn't kill Charles. He was fond of Charles." Her voice was measured—without expression.

Raleigh snapped impatiently, "Stop it, Naomi! You can't go to pieces now. The police will be here at the first moment they can make it. Sleep is what we all need. South will bounce back like a bad check. That's one of the reasons I came back here. He has my key and he'll figure it's the safest place to come."

Nora Gannon started to say something, but before she could more than get her lips open the door chimes sounded. She sat down abruptly.

Raleigh said, "Speak of the devil."

"No such luck—or bad luck," Nora said impatiently, and went to answer the door, switching on the hall light as she passed.

Naomi had started to tremble again. She adjusted the robe and hugged it closer, Chinese fashion.

It wasn't Joe. It was Thaddeus Davy, the district attorney. He was wet and on the verge of an explosion. Behind him a uniformed Homicide detective grasped Precious Lamb firmly by the arm. The maid looked solemn and unperturbed. She said, "Peace," as her eyes rested on the occupants of the room. The district attorney swore as he recognized Raleigh.

"Well, well," he greeted sarcastically. "A wake, as I live. I certainly am glad to see *you*." He didn't look it.

Raleigh said coldly, "This is no time to pun, Davy. You can begin by explaining what license you have to barge in here at four o'clock in the morning."

Davy's coldness matched the older man's. "My office carries a lot of license, Raleigh, and some aren't printed on paper. This girl was discovered trying to leave the city. We brought her back here for some questions before taking her to headquarters. Two birds with one stone. We hoped—just *hoped*, mind you—that Joe South would turn up here. Has he, Raleigh?"

The older man gave the district attorney credit for that one, but his own response was unworried. "That's better, Davy. Now that you're here you might as well finish what you started. *South is not here,* but don't let that stop you." He gestured toward the nurse. "This is my nurse, Miss Gannon. Miss Gannon, the district attorney, and my niece," he added shortly.

Thaddeus Davy nodded to the nurse and glowered toward Naomi. He said, "We've met."

The detective said, "What'll I do with this?" and shoved the maid forward.

"Oh, sit down and be quiet." Davy had the look of a man harassed beyond endurance. He didn't wait for an invitation but sat down heavily on the end of the davenport near the fire. His rimless glasses reflected light and made him look like a young schoolmaster trying to be stern. He glanced shrewdly at Raleigh. "Where is he?" he snapped.

"Where's who?" Raleigh countered.

"You know perfectly well whom I mean. Joe South. The entire police department has been . . ."

". . . searching for Joe South, private detective . . ." Precious Lamb chanted. The detective stopped her with a hand over her mouth. He swore and jerked it away as her teeth cut into his little finger.

"She's been reading your statements to the press, Davy," Raleigh said. "Don't blame her."

"I didn't know she could read," the policeman growled.

"Oh yes," Naomi put in irrelevantly. "Precious is studying for her doctor's degree in science at Columbia."

"Well, she can do her home work in the can," the policeman grunted and sat down.

"You didn't answer my question," Davy reminded Raleigh.

"What makes you think *I* know where South is?" Raleigh snapped irritably.

"He's working for you, isn't he?"

"What do you mean?"

"Oh, we hear things. What do you think a district attorney's job is, anyway?"

"Trying to put the Chief Executive in the bread line," Nora Gannon said solemnly.

Davy glowered. He said, "All this may be a joke to you people, Raleigh. It isn't to me. The police are skidding hellbent for nowhere and the citizens of this county are demanding action. They're going to get it. *I want South.* That, Raleigh, is why I'm here. And . . ."

He was interrupted by the ringing of the telephone. He reached the extension before the nurse was halfway out of her chair. He picked up the receiver and listened. When he recognized the caller, he said, "Yes, Davy speaking. . . . You *have?* Good, bring them

103

along. Yes, they're here . . . All right, hustle over." He hung up and went back to his chair. There was a satisfied smile on his face.

"Now, maybe we'll get somewhere. That was Sergeant Malone. He's rounded up' Van Pelt and his secretary." He smiled nastily. "They'll be over; along with some extra special guests. Frankie Shasta and Hyman Wiener, *and* a little surprise for you."

Raleigh said, "Nothing will surprise me any more."

The ear-splitting shriek of a police siren cut through the booming of the storm and ceased almost as suddenly as it had begun. The detective released his hold on Precious Lamb and strode belligerently to the door. When he returned he was followed by Sergeant Malone, Stuyvesant Van Pelt and Martha Lane. The lawyer, unperturbed and dapper as usual, came in with the secretary on his arm. It wasn't all affection. She needed support. At their heels Frankie Shasta sauntered easily. Porky Wiener waddled at his side, looking like Porky Wiener.

Sergeant Malone paused in the doorway and glanced apprehensively toward the hallway. Angry voices, and choice cuss words flavored the air. Before he could speak a red-faced policeman in plain clothes brushed by him. He was partially supporting, partially dragging a hotly protesting woman—or what looked like a woman.

She wore a dingy black coat fastened at the throat with a safety pin. Askew on her head was a weird black shape that passed for a hat. She carried a large patent shopping bag and an ancient umbrella sadly the worse for its tussle with the wind. She was still muttering angrily in the grasp of the embarrassed policeman.

"My gosh, what have you got there?" Davy goggled.

Raleigh said dryly, "The surprise, I presume."

Sergeant Malone looked indignant. He said, "She sees this Limey, Carton, and Joe South coming out of the Tomorrow Club. She comes back to see what's cooking after my men gets there. We picks her up on suspicion."

"How did she know it was South?" Davy was relaxing.

"She says they bumps into her and one of the guys has a stagey lingo."

"Very smart, Malone," Davy complimented him.

Raleigh said, "Get on with it, Davy."

Van Pelt spoke for the first time. "I thought you were in the hospital, Parker."

"So did Davy, apparently," he snapped.

Davy shifted his attention to the lawyer. He looked at him through narrowed eyes. "I'm after South."

"Yes, I know. I read the papers occasionally," Van Pelt was unperturbed.

Davy was getting mad. "Van Pelt, you have something up your sleeve, and all I can do at the moment is to take your word. But, I tell you this, even if you don't know where he is, you could put your hand on him if you wanted to. And if he isn't in my custody within twenty-four hours I'll have you behind bars for obstructing justice. Just think that over."

"From your action in the *last* twenty-four hours," said the lawyer smoothly, "it looks like I will have plenty of company."

The barb made its mark, and Davy turned on Shasta.

"We'll start from the beginning, Shasta. *Where is Joe South?*"

The racketeer's expression didn't change. "If you want to know where can I find Meester Sout', the answer is no! I too would like to talk wit' Meester Sout'. I would like he should tell me where is da ten t'ousan' dollar."

Davy groaned. "There you go again. Ten thousand dollars! That's all I've heard since we got hold of you and your corn-fed pal. I don't believe that yarn you've been handing us, so cut it out and tell me what you and Wiener were doing here the night the Evans girl was killed."

Shasta shrubbed. If Joe could have seen him he'd have sympathized. Without the inevitable pencil Shasta's long fingers were picking his tie to shreds. He said between tight lips, "I have tol' da poleece many time I come to meet Dicky. I hear shooting and I get lak hell away. I don' come inside da house. All I want ees da money. I don' wish harm to leetle Meely. I don' keel," he added briefly.

Davy looked apoplectic. "Don't talk, dago. But I'm giving you fair warning. We stay right here till I get action if it takes all night. This is only the beginning."

The wind came again and slashed rain against the windows. Staccato sound cracked like bullets as limbs ripped from trees, and the measured moan of fog-horns beat on tense nerves.

In a moment of silence a vicious blast shook the building. Every light went out. Startled gasps cut into the darkness. A wide triangle of light from Sergeant Malone's flash swept the room. It was joined by the homicide detective's smaller one. The bright glow from the fire shadowed faces into queer shapes and for a suspended second the room became a chamber of horrors.

Raleigh said, "A fuse must have gone."

The two policemen swore simultaneously. Precious Lamb said, "I'll get candles." She started for the door, the police escort at her heels.

"Better muzzle her," Davy advised with heavy wit. "This just about makes things perfect. South can walk down Fifth Avenue thumbing his nose at the police. They'll have their hands full now all right."

Nora Gannon shuddered. "I don't like this!"

Naomi hugged the robe closer. The room was charged and tense. Waiting. The sound of the hall door opening made everybody jump. Precious Lamb and the policeman entered, each bearing two candles like solemn acolytes at their first ceremony. The flames lightened the room and made shadows leap like queer-shaped bats. The storm roared and howled, and subsided with uncanny suddenness into a momentary lull. Then, as though it had been waiting, into the eerie silence another sound slithered and grew louder. It was a police siren.

"What the hell!" Thaddeus Davy was at the door before the chimes ceased. He threw it open into the startled faces of the six wilted figures on the steps.

Lieutenant Murphy?" he gasped. "What *have* you got there? This isn't a night court."

"The desk sergeant said I'd find you here, Mr. Davy," the lieutenant said triumphantly.

"Well, I'm here. So what?" Davy was sarcastic. He scowled. "I told you I wanted Joe South, not his drunken playmates," he added as he recognized Carton and Kierney. "And who is that?" He pointed to May.

"*Miss* Sands," Lieutenant Murphy stepped back. "We found these three but the prize had flown."

"All right, all right. Don't get poetic. Come in. We're having high tea."

They filed solemnly into the room behind him.

"Geeze, it *is* a party, Kitch." Kierney looked awed.

"As I live, all old friends together," Carton grinned as he caught sight of Shasta and Wiener.

"Cut the comedy!" Murphy snapped.

"Who are these people, Davy?" Raleigh demanded.

The district attorney's answer was cut short by the telephone. Davy grabbed the instrument. His face brightened as an excited voice buzzed his ear.

"Okay," he said with deceptive calm. "Bring him along." He hung up and turned on the waiting assembly. "It's the beginning of the last act, ladies and gentlemen. They've caught Joe South. *Now*, maybe we'll get some action into the script."

Carton, who had started to sit down beside May on the piano seat, helped her as she slumped quietly against him.

Chapter Thirteen

TWENTY MINUTES EARLIER Pete had pulled up on Prospect Place and parked his dripping cab near the entrance to Gloucester Tower. Joe started to get out. Two men who had been standing just inside the swinging doors, came toward them. Joe recognized them immediately. He dropped the brief case on the floor boards at Pete's feet and whispered hoarsely, "Hang on to that. Keep close."

Pete pushed the brief case under his feet. Joe stepped out into the barrel of a businesslike revolver. The man behind it said to Pete, "Get moving, buddy, and keep your trap shut. We'll look after your pal."

The driver spat from the side of his mouth and shrugged. "Okay, big shot. But he ain't no pal o' mine." He pressed the starter.

Rain swept Prospect and washed rivulets around Joe's ankles as he plodded ahead of the big policeman with the gun. He was wet and cold and unhappy. Icefloes started another jam in his stomach and he could no longer identify his head as his own. His brain was already shaken into a cocktail. The warmth of the lobby didn't help and he struggled to focus his gaze on the man with the gun. He said, "Is this a pinch?"

The policeman grinned. "Yes and no. We needed a fourth for bridge. You know how it is."

Joe sneezed. It didn't clear his head. He pulled his mind back with an effort. To keep on his feet until he saw the D. A.—that would be the job. If they got him in a cell he'd end up in the hospital. The last lap. After that the eight ball.

The policeman with the gun pushed him into one of the upright seats near the door.

"Keep an eye on him, Jerry," he ordered. "I got to call Murphy."

Joe tried to relax. His nerves screamed protest. Weariness twisted his eyeballs and beds leered at him from every corner of the lobby. One in a cell would have been welcome now. The thought of May and the brief case steadied him.

Wind-slapped water filled the street. It was louder now; more nerve-racking like stage effects beaten on a drum. His stomach tried to turn over. His skin felt tight and hot. He sneezed again and the ox-like policeman said solemnly, "Gesundheit!"

Sensation fled. He was floating through space. His head withdrew itself from his body and started a meaningless dance around his shoulders. A noose was being pulled under his chin. The voice of the policeman who had gone to telephone brought him out of it.

"The D. A.'s holding a little party at the Raleigh house," he told Jerry. "He's asked us to drop in."

Joe staggered in front of the two men into the angry storm. The ear at the curb was a cruising radio coupé and he was grateful to sit between them.

Jerry said, "Geeze, these killers is cold."

"Yeah. Remember the time I took 'Baby Face' Malloy up the river? Slept all the way like he hadn't just carved his woman up."

"You can't ever tell," Jerry wagged his head. "This guy here now. Shoots up half Manhattan. Then goes to sleep when he walks into us. I'm tellin' you. Some killers is cold . . ."

Joe was only dimly conscious of their voices. Now that he was going to see Thaddeus Davey before they took him to headquarters he had at least a fighting chance. If he could keep his head clear he'd be all right. He hoped the D. A. hadn't let reporters in.

The police car turned right at 78th Street. A half block farther on it jerked to a stop in front of the Raleigh house. Under lowered shades Joe saw people in a room. The policeman at the wheel got out and opened the door.

"All right, shamus. Don't try nothin' funny. Everybody'll like you better with a hole in your guts."

Joe didn't answer. They reached the door just as it was thrown open by the district attorney.

"Excellent work, Doheny," he greeted the man with the gun enthusiastically. He led them into the room. It looked like Macy's main aisle as Joe blinked dazedly in the candle light. Sergeant Malone was poking at a stubborn fire. He and Lieutenant Murphy looked at Joe grimly.

In a corner, alone, Precious Lamb stared into space, her chiseled face a bronzed blank. Her mind was occupied halfway between Harlem and Krum Elbow. She was lost without her police escort. There were now no policemen except Sergeant Malone and Lieutenant Murphy. Joe looked around anxiously until his eyes found May. She and Carton were straddling the long piano bench with a backgammon board between them, apparently absorbed in the game. They both smiled at him. Carton lifted his right hand and said "Cheer-o," then went back to the game.

Joe noticed that though May's lips were red, her face was pale and her eyes had blue shadows under them. His gaze traveled around the room and rested on Shasta who lounged against a window column, his dark eyes brooding and sullen. Porky Wiener was lumped on the wide ledge near him looking like a side of pork waiting for the butcher. His expression was the same as when Joe had first seen him. Stuyvesant Van Pelt and Martha Lane sat close together on a museum-piece love seat which had been moved away from the candle light. To the right of Sergeant Malone and nearer the fire, Nora Gannon was arranging a blanket over Raleigh's knees. As she saw Joe she gave the blanket a final pat and returned to the ottoman.

Naomi Raleigh huddled on the end of the davenport nearest her uncle and Joe noticed that even in the quilted robe with her hair touseled she still looked Fifth Avenue.

By the piano, stretched prone on the floor with a pillow under his head, Kierney was fast asleep. Joe knew all but one. The exception was the woman with the black umbrella. She had been goggling at him since he entered, and as Doheny led him nearer the fire she suddenly screamed, "That's him! That's the other one!"

Thaddeus Davy sat down in the vacant place on the davenport and Doheny pushed Joe toward him.

"There's your killer, Mr. Davy," he announced briefly.

"Sure this is the man?" Davy addressed the woman.

She came forward belligerently and thrust a finger under Joe's nose.

"Am I sure?" she shouted. "Of course I'm sure. I ain't blind and I didn't come here to be insulted."

Joe blinked sleepily and resisted the temptation to bite the dirty finger. He asked, "Of what?"

She flung out an arm and her voice rose hysterically, "You and that guy with the up-stage accent come out of that fancy place tonight. I seen you."

Joe said, "You don't say?" and wavered drunkenly.

Sergeant Malone grabbed his arm. He said, "Sit down, clown guy."

Joe weaved over, shoved the backgammon board from the piano seat and slid between May and Carton. He turned to May weakly. "I'm sorry I got you into this, honey."

Carton swung around, fingered a practiced chord on the key-board and ended with a crash. May touched Joe's hand.

"Don't worry about me, you alcoholic Sherlock. Start worrying about yourself. These gentlemen have you figured for a one-way excursion up the river with me for a publicity angle."

Joe looked around. "No reporters?" he asked sarcastically.

Sergeant Malone came toward him frowning heavily.

"Listen, buddy. You ain't here for a song and dance. Start talking business quick. We ain't got much time."

Joe grinned at Martha Lane. The district attorney motioned the sergeant to silence. Carton answered Joe's question as though no one else had spoken. He said, "The reporters are on their way, but the bobbies won't let them in. Not yet."

Joe looked at the district attorney. "What's holding you up, gang-buster? Not sure of your ground?"

Davy was whispering to Malone. Doheny was watching Joe. Joe

watched Frankie Shasta. Shasta was wearing a light gray suit.

Davy said, "South, on the basis of evidence submitted we find it necessary to arrest you for the murders of Richard Raleigh, Mildred Evans and Charles Shermond, pending further investigation, of course."

It didn't surprise Joe. He was still watching Shasta. He said, "That won't be necessary. There won't need to be any more investigation. You can bring your charge today, but not against me."

Van Pelt raised a warning hand. He said, "Careful, Joe. Don't invite a libel suit."

Joe said, "Libel, my . . ."

May stopped him. Joe got up. He said through a sneeze. "I'm tired and I don't feel like doing a B-picture fadeout. I've got a simple story if you'll gimme the stage, Davy, I'll go into my act."

Davy glanced at his watch. He said, "South, that's exactly what we're here for. You'll save some trouble with a confession . . ."

"Skip it," Joe said feebly. His eyes were watery. He turned to Lieutenant Murphy. "What've you got, Murphy? Suppose you give it to me without the dressing."

Wind came up and pumped the heavy drapes. A shutter banged. Murphy looked at the district attorney who nodded.

"All right, South. How's this? Mildred Evans got wise to your business. You had a quarrel with her at the Timbuctoo. You learned Richard Raleigh was carrying a bunch of money. You followed him home after pretending to be doped." The lieutenant smiled grimly "Oh yes, your two friends, Wiener and Shasta, were very helpful. You killed Raleigh, and the girl saw it. Then you killed her to keep her quiet. We found your bathrobe with blood on one of the sleeves. Add to that, a few minutes after Charles Shermond was killed, this woman here saw you and Carton leaving the Tomorrow Club. Oh no! We haven't much!"

Thaddeus Davy sat back and looked at the homicide man approvingly. He said, "We don't claim we have absolute proof, South, but enough to hold you for the Grand Jury."

Joe said, "How about the gun? Have you located it yet?"

Murphy shifted uneasily. He tried to cover it with bravado. "That's easy, South. *You're* going to tell us where that is."

A sick thought contracted Joe's diaphragm. Davy didn't miss the worried frown. He said, "That hits you where it hurts, doesn't it, South?"

Joe said, "It might, but it doesn't. Carton knows I didn't have a gun when we went to the Tomorrow Club. He also knows Shermond was dead when we got there."

Murphy looked at Carton accusingly.

"You too, huh, Limey?"

Carton grinned. He was feeling better. He patted May's hand. She was also smiling.

"How did you happen to be at the Tomorrow Club so conveniently, South?" Davy shot at the detective.

Joe was weary. "You won't believe me. Shermond called me at Miss Sands' apartment. He wanted to give me a message. As I started to hang up I heard two shots. Carton and I got there as quickly as we could. We found him dead. I dialed headquarters and left the receiver off the hook. Then I got the hell out."

Joe tossed an envelope to Davy. "Try that on your bazooka. It's the slug from the shot that missed Shermond." His grin was weak. "When you walk into the gun, just call me up and I'll come over and explain what to do with it."

Murphy glared. Joe was trying to look nonchalant. He said, "Does that help any, Davy?" He hoped his voice was steady.

"Keep talking, South. You'll have to do better than that to convince me my case isn't a good one."

"You're tough to crack, Davy." Joe was disgusted. "But you couldn't hold me long and you know it."

"Oh, couldn't I?" Davy was polite.

"No, I'm just a broken-down shamus to you, but when I'm through you'll have enough proof to start a rogues' gallery. Mr. Raleigh and Van Pelt hired me. They have a couple of strings on this fiddle. They'll listen."

Davy smiled, but his voice was still stubborn.

"I wouldn't let that worry me," he said quietly. "I've not exactly been idle and a job's a job no matter what it involves. I won't let *anyone* stop me, South."

Joe had to admit that this was true. Thaddeus Davy wouldn't resort to compromise.

"Okay," he said evenly. "You've a job to do. I've a job to do. Let's do it."

Joe looked around the room.

"Your case is full of holes. We'll skip that. When I'm through all the dotted lines will be filled in. I *was* drugged that night in Harlem. Milly was dead when I found her. Richard had been on the slab quite a time before I heard about it. I played the little man who wasn't there for obvious reasons." He brushed a hand across his eyes.

Davy looked bland. Murphy leaned against the mantel and watched Joe pityingly. Carton grinned and said, "Stout fella!" May moved closer to Joe. She said, "You'd better know what you're talking about, Phile. I'd about decided to take you up on that proposition."

Joe gave her a weak grin. Wiener grunted and shifted his position.

The detective stared at him as he would have if the sphinx had spoken. It was the first time he'd ever heard the fat boy make a sound. Shasta hissed, "What did you do wit' da money, Meester Sout'?"

Nobody paid any attention. Van Pelt said, "I always knew you had something, Joe."

"Da ten t'ousan' dollar, yes-s-s," Shasta said briefly.

Murphy looked at him sourly. He said, "Pipe down, Muscle-insky. Let the bright boy say his piece."

Joe shivered. "Mr. Raleigh hired me to keep an eye on Richard. I took the job under the impression that all I had to do was to keep him from sailing paper boats in Second Avenue gutters. I didn't know that there were a few dirty dollars involved. Four million of them. If I had known the cards were marked I'd have played them differently. When I took the count in Harlem I thought Dicky was getting playful." He looked at the two racketeers. "When those two harmless-looking cobras started getting tough it dawned on me that instead of getting generous pay for a stooge job with Richard I was being underpaid to take the rap for something a hell of a lot more serious." He paused again and got a match from Carton. No one spoke while he lit the cigarette. He slipped the match into a tray and continued, "I was plenty mad when I got back here Monday night, and practically out on my pins. I look dopey, I know, but I walked flatfootedly into the sweetest little set-up for a frame any killer ever dreamed of. It was by the same dumb luck that I saw the killer make his escape. As a result I found Milly's body hours before it was intended to be found."

Sergeant Malone spat disgustedly. "Just like Terry and the Pirates, huh?"

Joe ignored him. He continued, "The set-up kicked me out of my coma—that's when I dressed and got the hell out."

Van Pelt shrugged back into the shadows. Naomi was watching Joe with admiration.

When he spoke again Joe's voice was hoarser. It was getting difficult for him to breathe. "I telephoned Carton and Kierney before I left the house, naturally expecting them to pick me up. Shasta and Wiener here turned up first, so I rode with them instead. They said they were looking for Richard Raleigh. You can imagine my surprise when I thought all the time he was with them. They wanted to know, among other things, why I had killed Mildred Evans." He blew smoke in the air and addressed Shasta. "Still think I killed her, Shasta?"

Davy glowered at the racketeer. "You knew she was dead?"

Shasta's glance shifted to the district attorney.

"Tony Siano." He didn't raise his voice. "He was wit' us in da car.

He go in da house when Dicky don' come out. He see Meester Sout' in da room wit' little Meely, an' come lak hal to tell us. We t'ink Meester Sout' keel her, an' we pick him up so maybe he tell us where Deeky ees." His eyes went back to Joe. He said in the same monotonous tone, "All I want to know den—all I want to know now—is what did you do wit' da money, Meester Sout'?"

"Oh," Joe sneezed. "Is that all? Well, we'll get around to that. Just when I thought these two gentlemen were about to take more drastic measures the marines turned up. Mr. Carton and Mr. Kierney. I'm afraid they were a little rough though, and soon got the situation well in hand. In fact, they were very rude. They took all Mr. Shasta's and Mr. Wiener's personal belongings away with them."

"But," Davy interrupted, "Sergeant Malone turned their personal property over to the department when we arrested them in the raid the other evening. That's when we found Richard's car keys on them."

Joe's eyes brightened. He actually managed a grin. "Unh-huh? I know." He turned to May. "Make a note of that, Babe. I could have told you that, Davy, but it's better you noticed it all by yourself." own. I know this, because I tried practically all of them the day I went back to the warehouse to return their money and stuff. Richard Raleigh's keys, let me repeat, were not in their possession until *the murderer took the trouble to plant 'em on them.* Clear?"

The District Attorney stared. "How do we know *you* didn't have He tried to give the district attorney a stern glare and succeeded only in looking drunker. "It's a funny thing, Davy. When my pals rescued me from a fate worse than death Monday night, we took charge of everything the boys had on them. Cleaned them out, in fact. Remember they'd just come from the Raleigh house not a half hour after Richard and Milly were killed. But, *we found no keys except their* the keys all the time and planted them yourself?"

"Oh, Lord!" Joe's voice sounded far away to him. "Do I have to draw you a blueprint? I've witnesses—clouds of witnesses!"

Lieutenant Murphy took him up. "Prove it!" he snapped.

Joe had been leaning against the piano keys. Now he bent forward and spoke with emphasis. "Don't look so threatening, Herr Himmler. That's one of the easy ones. We went to Miss Sands' apartment," he continued, "as the least likely place the police would look for us. Kierney had already borrowed a couple of bottles from Mr. Shasta's bonded stock, and what with the drinks we had at the Timbuctoo and a bottle I bagged from Van Pelt's office, it didn't take all day to learn it was all coming from the same cow. Add that up and even you'd come to the conclusion that Van Pelt knew a little more about Richard's peccadilloes than he'd originally led me to believe."

The lawyer cleared his throat and glowered at Joe. Naomi smiled encouragingly. Precious Lamb was asleep. Joe leaned back again with his elbows on the piano and crossed his legs.

"When I went back to the warehouse I also found out that Van Pelt had made a visit to his clients. That one was easy too. You don't need a slide rule for all the answers." He grinned at Van Pelt. "Anybody with his nose in a sling could smell those Havanas from across the river, Stuyvie." He sneezed again. "But I'm digressing. You all know about the will, so I'll skip all but the salient points which Mr. Van Pelt took great pains to point out." His voice was thickening and his throat felt tight and dry. He got up and wavered feebly toward Nora Gannon. Before anyone could stop him he had picked up her glass and finished the brandy. Still without interference he returned to his seat beside Carton. He said, "That's better," and coughed.

Nobody spoke. Joe's chest felt tight, as though Wiener's feet were resting on it. "I learned all these facts, little by little, from Van Pelt. And, incidentally, he was a little too anxious to remind me that Parker Raleigh's field of finance had been kicked into a cocked hat. He made nice neat blueprints of it all."

Van Pelt hadn't stirred. Parker Raleigh passed Nora a tired smile. Naomi was all ears. Joe started to take a cigarette, sneezed again and put the package back.

Thaddeus Davy said, "Let's have it, South. Who's on your ballot?"

"I haven't a ballot yet. It's obvious, or was to me, by that time, that Van Pelt was slipping out of character in his zeal for pointing out facts. An example was that he told me of his own free will and accord that both the prospective heirs were about to marry very much against their uncle's wishes. I'm trying to get over the idea that the bootleg racket had practically nothing to do with the motive for Dick's death—except in aiding the murderer to expedite his plans. It was when I uncovered a neat little blackmail plan Dick had concocted against Van Pelt that I was ready to accuse him of the murders. How about it, Van Pelt?"

Chapter Fourteen

MARTHA LANE broke the silence. "Somebody cart out that alcoholic maniac. If everybody must know, I was with Mr. Van Pelt every minute that night . . ."

The lawyer tried to stop her. She shrugged his hand off roughly. "No, don't interfere with me! I don't give a darn what people think. That burlesque Superman can't walk around tossing accusations like he does dirty cracks."

Joe smiled feebly. "There seems to be a lot of that going on around town. What *will* the '50 census show?"

Van Pelt's voice was steady. "Joe, I didn't give you credit for that much imagination. You know, of course, that you haven't a shred of evidence that would stand up before a jury."

Precious Lamb awakened long enough to say, "Peace." A little late, Joe thought. He said, "Plenty of evidence, Stuyvie. There's the marked bills, remember? And that bum liquor with the phony labels. Start laughing that off, Stuyvie."

Thaddeus Davy's voice was loud with sarcasm. "Would it be all right with you gentlemen if I got in on this? What bills?" He thundered.

Joe raised a hand shakily. "You guys have had a couple of days on this with plenty of help from the night shift. What did it get you? It got you me—and I was coming in anyway. I'm here to show you the page with the answers. Do I have the floor?"

Davy subsided. Joe continued. "You see, here was a young man who had been brought up with a string of greenbacks dangling in front of his eyes—but always just out of reach. They were there, but he couldn't play with them. He became bitterer and bitterer. It was natural for a boy with his temperament to work himself up into an attitude of 'I'll-show-them.' At first, he found it easy to borrow from Van Pelt, who was perfectly willing to line his opera coat with a little velvet in the nature of interest." He squinted at the lawyer. "How about it, Stuyvie? You do hold his notes, don't you?"

Van Pelt's expression didn't change. He said, "I'm not a fool, Joe."

"I didn't think you were," Joe conceded. "Well, this *debt* gradually developed into something over fifty thousand dollars over a period of less than two years. But Van Pelt was beginning to lecture Dick, and Dick wasn't strong on lecture periods. He still couldn't see why he shouldn't have a free hand. Then he met Mildred Evans, who, through her various jobs in night clubs, was on to all the tricks. I'm guessing now, but she must have put Dick onto Shasta and Wiener. They could use a good Social Register camouflage, and it was pie for Dick to get the job. How he came to suspect Van Pelt's connection with them I don't know." He nodded to the lawyer. "Maybe you could help us there, Stuyvie?"

Van Pelt was taking the punches like a veteran. He said grimly, "I didn't even suspect he knew, South, until you showed me those marked bills. They were a part of the last batch Shasta delivered. It didn't take me long to figure that Richard had been cooking up a blackmail scheme against me. When Naomi uncovered his connection with Wiener and Shasta I refused to lend him any more money unless he broke with them. I'm not quite the criminal you think I am."

Joe smiled. "So you admit it. I knew you were a smart boy,

Stuyvie."

"Smart?" Van Pelt lifted an eyebrow. "The rock pile at Alcatraz is much more comfortable than the electric chair."

Joe handed the district attorney one of the hundred-dollar bills. "Examine it," he suggested briefly.

Davy turned it over and peered more closely. "R. S. V. P.," he said. He looked at Joe blankly and returned the bill. "What does it mean?"

"Part of the record, Davy," Joe reminded him. "Those marked bills. Remember? Simple. Richard was collecting the money, marking it in a Dick Tracy attempt to get material evidence against Van Pelt, and then turning it over to Shasta. In plain United States those initials mean 'From Raleigh to Shasta to Van Pelt.' Simple?" He lifted a casual hand. "It doesn't take an engineer to add them apples, Davy. On the face of it, that should clear Van Pelt. All his careful arrows were pointing away from the racket to keep me diverted. He had no idea that there would be a tie-up there for a murder rap until I called his attention to the bills."

Davy swore. Lieutenant Murphy looked baffled, and Sergeant Malone had long since turned the whole business over to his superiors. Jerry and Doheny were goggling at the rabbits coming out of the hat.

"How do you know Richard marked those bills, Joe?" Davy found his voice.

"Duck soup." Joe was beginning to feel wobbly in the knees. May put her hand on his wrist. Her touch was cool. "I know he put them there because there was green ink in his fountain pen. Wiener can't write and Shasta uses an indelible pencil. Van Pelt wouldn't have any reason to do it. The bills were handled primarily by those four. No other answer. Richard put them there."

"And the rest of the money?" Davy asked softly. "It couldn't just disappear in thin air."

"It didn't," Joe snapped. "Wait." His gaze swept the circle of faces. Wiener and Shasta hadn't moved. A look of pained tensity darkened Nora Gannon's face and she had her hand on Raleigh's wrist. Kierney had gone back to sleep and Carton, who had retrieved the backgammon board, was rolling dice back and forth over its surface. Naomi was returning to normal. The maid was bored and the charwoman was snoring in a corner. Joe said, "One more favor, Davy. I'd like to see the kind of dough these people are toting. Have them turn their pockets out."

Davy nodded to Sergeant Malone and Joe waited while he collected wallets and hand-bags. Murmurs of protest mingled with the roll of the dice as Joe systematically began his examination. From Wiener's wallet he took a fifty-dollar note and placed it to one side. Shasta's held three hundred-dollar bills. He added these to the fat man's.

A brief glance inside Nora Gannon's modest purse revealed a single dollar bill and small change. Raleigh's wallet held two, fives and several coins. Van Pelt's handsome zippered folder yielded two hundreds which went into the pile with Wiener's. He pushed May's bag aside untouched and glanced at her. She smiled. The dog-eared billfold belonged to Kierney and he returned it unopened. The hundred-dollar bill from Carton's pigskin case went into the pile of larger denominations. He opened the red patent-leather bag the maid had laid quietly on the table, and returned it after a cursory glance inside. She grinned and closed her eyes again. Neither Naomi nor Martha Lane was carrying a purse, and he ignored the charwoman's dingy black one.

Kierney said, "Take my roll too, Joey. I'm still in the game." Joe frowned and gestured to Carton.

"How about that envelope, pal?" The Englishman tossed it to Joe and the detective placed it to one side.

Sergeant Malone scowled. "Looks like you and your pals is in the dough, South."

"Only a windfall, buddy," Joe croaked. "Davy, look at those bills. See the initials?"

Silently the district attorney and Lieutenant Murphy looked the bills over and nodded. Davy drew a long breath and said, "Your round, South. Roughly, though, there's only about five hundred dollars showing. You'll have to do better than that."

"I'm not walking into that one, Davy. This isn't the stolen money. Except this one." He tossed the single bill from the envelope to Davy. "You might keep that one apart for fingerprints. It's the one we took off Shermond this morning," Joe added blandly.

Murphy started toward him. "Ghouls too, huh?"

Naomi's interruption stopped the lieutenant. The musical break in her voice emphasized its sadness. "You needn't leave me out, Joe. Go on. Tell them. It doesn't make any difference now that Charles is dead."

Joe eyed her wearily. "I was coming to that, Naomi. You should find some consolation in the fact that there are others in your class." He nodded toward Martha Lane.

Shasta moved nearer the table. He pushed the money contemptuously. "Where is da ten t'ousan' dollar, Meester Sout'?"

Joe sighed resignedly. "Go play that disk on your own music box, Franco. You won't need it where you're going. That one-track mind of yours has already done you a favor. If you can call it that. Don't worry. I had you and your baby elephant figured in for a while. But you were both too convinced that I had kidnaped Richard. You'd never have taken the risk you did with me Tuesday morning if you'd just bumped the girl. That kind of rap for guys like you ain't worth a measly ten thousand dollars. All you were concerned with was getting the ten thousand dollars." He turned to the district attorney. "And if that's not enough to start on, Davy, you could see Wiener's girlfriend at the Timbuctoo. Tony Siano might come in handy too." He leered at the fat man. "Ponies from your own rodeo, eh, Porky? I never thought the day would come when I'd help clear you of a murder rap." Joe stopped to stare at the fat man fascinated. The faintest trace of a smile had rippled his jelly-like cheeks.

Joe blinked and the face wavered. He tried to focus the district attorney's eyes and gave it up. He spoke to the room at large. "Also those two haven't any Harvard degrees, but they've got better sense than to run around with a murdered man's keys in their pockets."

Davy looked nonplussed. Murphy spat into the fire.

Van Pelt said, "You'd better have proof, Joe."

"Proof?" Joe tried to snap, but his voice sounded like it was coming from the wrong end of a bazooka. "What are you worried about?" He tried again. "You and your thugs better start chewing another bone." He didn't wait for the lawyer's retort. He was looking at Parker Raleigh. "How about it, Raleigh?"

The sick man met Joe's eyes coldly. He said, "Keep it within limits, South. Make it brief."

"Okay. How long were you at the Timbuctoo the night Richard was killed?"

Van Pelt jerked upright. Naomi gasped, "Uncle Park!" Nora Gannon looked severe. Murphy groaned.

Parker Raleigh was unmoved. He said, "You're better than I thought, South. I was afraid you'd discovered it. How did you know where we went?"

Joe tossed the paper of matches on the table.

"These were in your topcoat. That's what happens when you don't talk. Thought you sent me off half-cocked, huh?" He coughed. "I had your motive and there was the opportunity made to order. You've been losing dough on the market; you've had access as co-trustee to a large trust fund. That is, until Richard married or came of age, at which time said fund would dwindle to half. With Richard out of the way, you were saved. But Naomi was still a monkey-wrench in the works. There had to be an accounting if she married. She was going to marry Shermond. The will stipulates that the remaining heir will inherit the income from the entire trust fund when the other dies—*if said living heir is married*. Now, in Naomi's case, she would have to wait five years before she had full control of the legacy in any event; *but,* in the meantime it wouldn't be easy for you to turn loose the income from four millions—not in your present reduced financial condition. You needed more time, so Shermond had to be got out of the way."

"Good gosh!" Raleigh had paled this time. "You do have a working imagination, don't you, South?"

Joe raised a shaking hand. "Wait a minute. How's your alibi for the night Richard was murdered?"

Nora Gannon got to her feet and faced Joe across the room. Raleigh spoke to her under his breath, but she shook her head.

"Mr. South," her voice was restrained, "if this is giving you any pleasure I hope you've had enough. Maybe it's your duty. I think this is my cue for a few words. No." She touched the sick man's lips with her fingers when he tried to interrupt. "It's time someone thought of you, Parker." She turned back to Joe. Her violet eyes, dark-fringed and brilliant, gazed straight at him. "Mr. Raleigh and I went to the Timbuctoo together the night Richard was killed. He was worried about Richard and he thought we'd find him there. As his nurse, I knew it would do him no harm. He was very ill for a few weeks from a nervous disorder brought on by overwork. He has actually been well enough to leave the hospital for the last week, but Dr. Roberts, his physician, advised him not to rush things. The doctor knew that he went with me, and where we went. He telephoned me at the Timbuctoo at eleven o'clock, and at two the three of us were having coffee in Dr. Roberts' office. The doctor will corroborate this, as will the Night Supervisor."

The nurse brushed a hand across her eyes. Parker Raleigh looked at her impatiently and pressed her hand. He said, "That was unnecessary, Nora. My innocence is its own proof."

"Innocent men have gone to the chair before, Raleigh," Joe reminded him. "Thank you, Miss Gannon. That clears up one point."

"And since Miss Gannon has gone that far"—Raleigh might have been chewing green persimmons—"for your further information, there's nothing whatever irregular in my taking her to the Timbuctoo. We are going to be married as soon as these tragedies have been cleared up."

Naomi's face brightened briefly. She said, "How marvelous for you, Uncle Park!"

Nora Gannon smiled at her. "Thank you, dear," she said simply, and turned back to Joe.

"Another thing which may help you, Mr. South. Mr. Raleigh is no longer a wealthy man, but I happen to know the children's fortune is intact." A slight flush colored her cheeks. She added with an effort, "I nursed Dick through pneumonia three years ago. When I told Mr. Raleigh I'd marry him, it was natural for him to take me into his confidence."

Van Pelt said unexpectedly, "She's quite right, Joe. The trust fund is in better shape than ever."

Joe said, "That helps." He felt light-headed and wished to heaven he was through. He sneezed and blew his nose noisily. When he could speak again, he said, "Looks like our suspects have run out, Davy."

"It still leaves you in, shamus," Sergeant Malone said truculently.

Davy rose and stood over Joe.

"South, I thought this was going to be simple. How much longer is it going on? Come to the point. We haven't the rest of the week. The money is still missing and so is this phantom murderer you had up your sleeve. You can't produce one with talk, and you haven't talked yourself out of the mess yet. For the last time—*where is that ten thousand dollars?*"

Joe managed a watery grin. "So he's got you doing it too?"

Murphy swore. "Skip the funny papers, South, and get back to facts!"

Joe raised a hand to silence the irate policeman.

"I'm coming to the end—in more ways than one," he added. His head was splitting and he had trouble separating words. "You want a motive. All cops want motives—all God's chillun want motives. All right—how do you like this one? Greed. Greed for money. Every road I came to had a detour sign with a dollar mark on the end. They all pointed to a four-million-dollar estate and ten thousand dollars that couldn't be found. But everybody involved wanted money—a lot of money. Who don't? Dick wanted it and got a hole in his belly. Milly wanted Dick on accounta she smelled money on him. Van Pelt, Martha Lane, Raleigh . . ." His voice trailed low. He felt numb. His feet wouldn't move and the eyes of the people in the room danced together and bored into his brain. Still tensity galvanized the air and he tried to catch his breath. Even the maid was staring at him as though he were the pea under the shell. He wavered against Carton.

May said, "He's ill!"

Murphy said, "Drunk, u mean!"

Joe said, "To hell with it," and mumbled to Carton, "Watch this!" He sat up straighter with a great effort and spoke to Sergeant Malone. "There's a cab out front. Go out and tell the driver to give you my bag."

His voice sounded loud in his ears. Without a word the sergeant obeyed.

Shasta cleared his throat. "Is it da ten t'ousan' dollar, Meester Sout'?"

Joe ignored him and concentrated his wavering sight on the dice Carton was still worrying. It seemed hours, but it was only a minute or two later that the sergeant returned. No one moved as he placed the briefcase on the table. Joe motioned the district attorney. "Open it," he directed.

Suddenly, without warning, he slid swiftly from the piano bench and reached the davenport in one stride. May screamed. There was a loud report. Blood spurted from Joe's right hand. He seized the gun with his left and threw it across the room. He thrust the shrieking, writhing figure in his arms toward the district attorney.

"Slap the cover on this, Davy," he croaked, and with his doubled fist caught Naomi Raleigh under the chin. She collapsed at his feet. "Hang on to that gun, Sergeant. That's the baby!"

Carton caught him as he sagged to the floor. He said gently, "Stout fella!"

━━━━━━━━━━ *Chapter Fifteen* ━━━━━━━━━━

JOE MOVED HIS HEAD. It felt like a bowl that had been used in the last Chicago tournament. He tried opening his eyes. He was in the hospital room with white leather chairs and tubular fixtures. It was the same all right. The one Raleigh had been in, and sun made the right kind of bars through the grilled windows. Its brightness made him dizzy and he closed his eyes. He felt empty. His mouth was dry and cottony. What he needed was food. He was pleased at the discovery. He reached up and pressed the button over his head.

The door opened almost immediately and a nurse came in. Joe stared. "Dr. Gannon, I presume." His voice was weak, but his grin made up for it.

Nora Gannon smiled. "How do you feel?"

"Ambitious," he said. "Which one of the skyscrapers hit me that time?"

"Not this time, Joe. Just a very small bug. Pneumonia. This is your tenth day." She put her hand on his wrist. "You can't run around soaking wet indefinitely with no sleep and no food and come up feeling like Tarzan." She frowned. "You're talking too much. It's time for your medicine."

Joe grinned. "All right, Miss Nightingale, I'll take it when you tell me what it's all about."

She came closer and made a face. "Starting already, eh? All right. Lesson Number One. Never get fresh with your nurse."

"When you say them words, smile, pardner," Joe chuckled. He gestured around the room. "The last time I was on a case a guy put me in the hospital with a razor. But all I remember this time is a bullet that didn't connect."

She pointed to his bandaged wrist. "That's what you think. It connected all right. And that's enough for now. See how this tastes." The teaspoon she thrust between his lips stopped his protest. "I'll see that you get something to eat. And if you'll stop trying to be an Eagle Scout you may have some visitors."

Joe swallowed the bitter liquid reluctantly. The nurse pulled the covers up and left the room. He stopped trying to keep his eyes open and slept. When he awoke again May was sitting beside the bed. She looked tired and there was moisture in her eyes. She said, "Hi, Sherlock," and smiled.

"Hi, babe. How'm I doin'?" His world righted itself. She looked good like she always did.

"They almost got you that time, didn't they? The bugs, I mean. I told you you should have had another hamburger."

She came nearer the bed. He reached for her hand.

"Am I sawing wood or did I really hear you call me 'darling'?" he asked gruffly.

"Nope, dope—but I will." She stooped and kissed him. "That's my answer, Joey. Remember? You picked yourself more than trouble when you propositioned *me*. In about a minute you're going to have some important visitors. Be quick with your wooing. Everybody's terribly grateful. Even the shanty-town boys. Look at this." She pulled a small stand nearer the bed. On it was a giant horseshoe wreath of assorted flowers, tied to one prong of which was a large white ribbon. She handed him the card which had been attached to the other one. On one side was written in old-fashioned copperplate script, "To a good guy with apologies. Over." Joe twisted it around. It said, "I *can* write too. Wiener."

He grinned. "Baby, it was worth being sick to get a rise out of fat boy."

Voices came through the open transom. A moment later the door opened. Carton and Kierney entered. Thaddeus Davy and Parker Raleigh brought up the rear. The handsome face of the latter had lost none of its steel, but there were new lines around his lips, and his shoulders drooped.

Carton said, "It's time you were stirring. Your public's getting impatient. The newspaper chaps have had a Roman holiday. I warn you, though. Your life won't be worth a ha'penny once you get out. They're gunning for you for giving up and dying right before press time."

Kierney was carrying a package which he placed solemnly on Joe's chest.

"There y'are, Joey. A whole quart of rye. The McCoy too." He stood back and surveyed Joe with satisfaction.

Joe said, "Thanks, guy. Take a pew everybody."

Parker Raleigh and the district attorney sat down awkwardly, as visitors do in hospitals. Raleigh said, "Joe, I shan't try to thank you. You know how I feel. Davy and I wanted to pay our respects, and Davy wants to get a few details straightened out. That is, if you feel up to it."

"Shoot," Joe grinned at Nora Gannon. "Orders from headquarters," he reminded her. "I'll be glad to fill in the gaps if I can, Davy. I suppose her confession is in order."

"Oh yes," Davy looked at Raleigh and hesitated.

The older man brushed a hand across his eyes. "Don't mind me, Davy. I'm still stunned. I feel as though all this were happening to someone else."

"I'm sorry, Raleigh." The district attorney's eyes were troubled. "It's a bad business any way you look at it. But with what Joe has I hope our case will be complete."

"Glad to oblige," Joe assured him. He leaned back against the pillows. He was weak but at peace with the world. "It seemed simple enough once I got all the ends picked up. The girl was lucky and clever and had a lot of luck. If I'd had my wits about me I'd have guessed sooner that the whole thing hinged on the will. But there were too many fingers in the pie. I couldn't see the trees for the forest." He gestured toward Raleigh. "Would you mind giving us the gist of the will just to keep the record straight?"

"If it will help," Raleigh said briefly. "Maybe if I'd been a little more explicit a good deal of this wouldn't have happened. You see, when Dick died, his share automatically became Naomi's. The fact that she wouldn't inherit hers until she was thirty, or five years after her marriage, made it seem unlikely that she'd have any reason to get rid of Richard. Her allowance of two thousand dollars was to be increased to five thousand the minute she married. In the meantime, if anything happened to Richard the income from the entire trust fund would be hers immediately. Add to that the fact that once

Richard was married, Naomi lost all chance of getting anything more than a substantial increase in her allowance until she was thirty, and you have a dangerous situation."

"There you have it," Joe observed. "She first walked into the suspect column when Miss Sands wanted to know how she could afford the kind of clothes and jewels she wore on two thousand a year. Then it dawned on me that she was probably not marrying Shermond just for love, and I started giving her more attention. He was a perfect tool for her plans. Weak-kneed, vague and concerned only with his own ambitions. When he had served her purpose she could have unloaded him without a squeak."

Davy said, "She wasn't missing any tricks."

"Oh, no," Joe agreed. "She was in Van Pelt's office the afternoon he hired me. She kept tabs on my movements from then on. She knew I'd find Dick at the Timbuctoo and she followed me there. Whether or not she had intended to act that evening I don't know. But events there and later in Harlem climbed right up in her lap. Dick's announcement that he and Milly were planning to get married at once was his death warrant. She couldn't afford to give him a chance to marry the girl. She made her plans quickly. Their success depended upon blitzkrieg methods."

Carton moved from the window and sat on the edge of the bed.

"Then it was *she* who doped your drink instead of Richard?"

"Unh-huh. But it took me quite awhile to tumble to that. A while and nearly a bottle of Scotch." He recounted his ride with Pete and his sudden memory of the conversation between Mildred and Richard before he passed out on the Mickey Finn. "I knew that what he said then was off the record. He really thought I was out from the whisky I'd drunk, and had no idea that I'd been doped. That left only one answer. Naomi. It was like knocking over a row of dominos then. Everything fell into place, and my next move was to find the money. Without it I had no material proof to confront her with. I tried to telephone her at the Gramercy park apartment. It was ducky for me that she'd already left. I don't know what I'd have done if she'd been there." He grinned at Carton. "My key man wasn't handy, so I did the next best thing—pushed the door in with the fire ax—during the height of the storm, remember? It was there, all right. Sandwiched in the mattress of the folding bed in the living room."

Nora Gannon moved nearer the bed. "All right, Joe. Make it snappy. You're talking too much as it is."

Davy said apologetically. "I'm sorry, Joe. I'll finish for you. After she doped your drink she took Shermond back to the apartment, doped his coffee, put on his clothes and drove back to the Raleigh house. She had overheard Richard tell the Evans girl that he had to meet the boys in his garage at a later hour to turn over the collections.

"She got to the garage just as Richard was putting his car away. She naturally assumed he was just coming in. As a matter of fact, he had already put a drunken Mildred to bed and was waiting to deliver the money to the boys. She was cutting her time short, and she let him have it without even speaking to him. She took his keys along with the brief case. Her greedy mind couldn't picture leaving it there, and its absence might be attributed to robbery."

Joe said, "Yeah. I figured it was something like that. Mildred Evans must have heard something. Dick's bedroom overlooks the garage. She probably looked out and saw Naomi closing the doors. In her fright she turned on the light and rushed into the hall to telephone. Her fingerprints on the upstairs extension suggests that."

"But she was killed in bed, Joe," Carton observed.

"Sure she was," Davy took it up again. "Naomi says Mildred had already lifted the receiver down. She hadn't even put on a dressing gown. When she saw Naomi with a gun, in her drunken condition she didn't recognize her in men's clothes and she fainted. Naomi dragged her back to Dick's bed, pulled the covers up, slipped the gun against her stomach and mashed the trigger. All this delayed her. When she heard Joe's ring she slipped down the back stairs to the rear exit in time to stand behind the door as Joe entered. She didn't dare try to get to the back fence until she was sure Joe had gone to bed. She was still there when she heard Shasta's car. She guessed who it was and had to take a chance. That was when Joe saw her go over the fence."

Joe said, "Then she hurried back to Gramercy Park and deliberately put the car in a different place."

"You guessed that, did you?"

"Not all guessing, Davy. I found the parking ticket on Shermond when Carton and I searched him right after he was shot. If the car had been parked in one place from the time she said they got back, the time checked would have been earlier than six o'clock. Another red-herring for the police."

"That's why she killed Shermond," Davy continued. "He got suspicious and was trying to telephone Joe when she shot him. She had tried to bribe him and after she shot him she deliberately left the marked bill to confuse the police further."

"She sure had luck," Joe mused. "She could hardly have been undressed from that little murder when those homicide men turned up in a routine check up looking for me. They hadn't had time to learn of Shermond's death, and she didn't waste time getting away from there after they left, not forgetting to bring along the handy little shootin' iron."

"How about the dope?" Nora put in. "Did you find where she was getting it?"

"Not yet. It probably comes from the usual bootleg source. We haven't been able to get that out of her yet. She has nothing to lose by keeping her mouth shut and she's like all the rest—she's afraid if she gives it away she'll never to be to get more if she wriggles out of this rap." The district attorney looked grim. "*If* she does."

Joe looked at Kierney who had gone to sleep in the most comfortable chair in the room. He yawned.

"It was lucky for me you had all those people out there that night, Davy. My pins wouldn't have lasted much longer."

The district attorney smiled. "The department has to earn its salary, Joe. And don't forget we had some mighty damaging evidence stacked against you."

Joe raised an eyebrow. "Are you telling I? But that was exactly what she wanted. It didn't make much difference who was suspected as long as she was in the clear. She must not have had much hope that suspicion against Wiener and Shasta would go far, yet she took the trouble to plant those keys in Wiener's pocket right under my nose." Joe's eyes were serious for a moment. "One of my chief regrets is that I couldn't save Shermond."

The district attorney frowned. "Yes, you fell down there, Joe. You should have called the police."

"The police!" Joe scoffed. "I didn't have time. Besides they'd have slapped me in the jug." Suddenly he jerked up in bed, and fell back as quickly. "Good gosh!" he shouted. "Has anybody seen Peter? I must owe that guy a fortune!"

"Don't worry, Joe," May calmed him. "He's gunning for you. He calls every day to know how you are. This morning he said he hoped you'd remember him in your will."

"Good old Pete," Joe sighed. "What did you do with Van Pelt and his playmates?" he asked Davy.

The district attorney smiled. "Don't lose too much sleep over them. The Federal men already had them tagged. But if Van Pelt doesn't get himself and company out by Easter he isn't the lawyer I think he is."

Nora Gannon said, "All right, Joe. Time's up. You'll talk yourself into an iron lung."

Raleigh rose and stood by the bed. "Yes," he agreed. "We wouldn't want that. Here's my check, Joe." He handed the detective a folded slip of paper. "It isn't much for what you've done. You know I'm grateful. If there's ever anything else I can do, don't hesitate."

Joe took the extended hand and slid the check under his pillow. He felt sorry for Raleigh, but he knew Nora would fix that. Carton rose, and held out his hand.

"We'll see you soon, boy. Good luck." He turned to Kierney. "Coming, Mick?"

"Yeah. See you in church, Joey." Joe grinned happily as the door closed on the two men.

Davy stood by the bed and extended his hand with a friendly smile.

"We appreciate your help, Joe. But next time we'd like a little more co-operation. The police aren't such bad working mates, after all." He looked embarrassed. "And, by the way. Drop around when you're out and let's see what we can do about that license."

Joe said, "Yeah," and turned to May as the door closed behind the district attorney and Parker Raleigh. She had risen and was pulling on her gloves.

"I must go too, Joey. You've had enough for one day. I'll see you tomorrow." She stooped and kissed him lightly on the lips. His good arm went about her shoulders.

"Oh, no you don't, Babe. How's about that proposition?"

This time the pressure of her lips wasn't light. When she pulled away her lovely skin was suffused with pink.

"Joey, you do take advantage of a girl, don't you? I said yes, and I mean yes. Now will you be good? I must go." And she was gone before he could protest. The fragrance of spring that she always seemed to carry about lingered.

Joe leaned back against the pillows. He raised his wrist for the time and remembered his watch was still missing. Sunshine streamed through the windows, and a brisk December breeze ruffled the curtains. He pondered the last time he had sat in this room and watched a storm's fury, wishing he were in Raleigh's shoes. He didn't now He was very tired. He closed his eyes and opened them suddenly as the door clicked. Pete stood there looking awkward and uncertain in the unfamiliar surroundings.

Pete's homely features were troubled. He moved slowly to the bed. "Joey, you all right?" he whispered sepulchrally.

"No, dope. I'm dead and buried. Just lay those forget-me-nots on the tombstone." He reached under the pillow and brought out the check which he had not yet unfolded. Solemnly he handed it to Pete. "Here's your dough, dope."

Pete opened it and let out an oath that could have been heard in the operating room.

"For cripe's sake, Joey! Ten thousand dollars! Who d'ya think I'm workin' for—Br-r . . . ?"

Joe grabbed the check from the driver's hand. He snapped, "Gimme that." One glance and he fell back with a thud. The figure was right!

THE END

www.ingramcontent.com/pod-product-compliance
Lightning Source LLC
Chambersburg PA
CBHW020656180626
46816CB00003B/1317